THE HAPPY BAKER

A Girl's Guide to Emotional Baking

by Erin Bolger

HARLEQUIN®

THE HAPPY BAKER

ISBN-13: 978-0-373-89241-9

Creative Design and Direction – Erin Bolger
Art Direction – Sandy Peic @ Inspired Sight & Sound Inc.
Cover and Book Design – Sandy Peic @ Inspired Sight & Sound Inc.
Editor – Carla Lucchetta
Illustrator – Erin Bolger
Food Photography – Jason Hervey
Prop Stylist – Eden Bluestein
Food Stylist – Erin Bolger
Hand Model – Nikki Rae
Bedazzler – Jenia O'Connor
Author Photo – Richard Dubois Photography
Author Hair – Danielle Williams

www.eHarlequin.com

Printed in U.S.A.

Dedicated to every man
who has broken, bruised
or made my heart ache (either good or bad)...

Dedicated to my mom.

And everyone who has enjoyed my baking
and countless dating stories over the years.

The stories in my book are inspired by events in my life.
Vodka may have been involved while writing them.
My intent is to write humorous relatable stories,
not to bash the men I have encountered...
seriously.

INTRODUCTION

My Name is Earl meets *Sex and the City* meets "Grandma's Cookie Jar."
Yep, that's my book in a nutshell, possibly with a little *Golden Girls* thrown in…think Rose Nylund.

circa 1984

circa a much better year

The Happy Baker book is a collection of recipes of which most are unique to my rural upbringing, matched with my personal dating memories. The memoir vignettes are singularly my own but are at the same time very relatable. Sometimes it's nice to know you weren't the only one to make out with a long-haired rocker in the middle of a cornfield, with bangs the size of Oklahoma!

I am part country, part city…and all woman. After living for eighteen years in a village of nine hundred people, I thought it was time to tackle the Big Smoke aka Toronto, Canada's answer to N.Y.C.! I spent two years taking a cosmetics program there. Being a makeup artist for the last thirteen years has been quite successful for me. Most people might wonder what a professional makeup artist is doing writing a chick-lit cookbook. But, baking has come as naturally to me as makeup artistry has. When you've got passion, anything is possible. If they gave out degrees for sugar addictions, I would be on the honor roll.

My writing career started at the fall fair, in public school. I am the proud recipient of many first- and second-place ribbons for creative writing. If you saw the way they judge a pumpkin, you would know why. The idea for this book hit me like a ton of bricks. I couldn't have stopped writing if I'd tried. I would have written in my sleep if possible. I even got writer's arm (definition: a tan on one arm from writing outside all day).

I love to bake and I love to tell stories. I can't tell you how many times I've heard, "Erin, you should write a book." Well, here it is. The recipes are easy to follow, with ingredients that are easy to find. Dating is hard enough, so I figure your emotional baking shouldn't be. Since the recipes are my personal favorites, they are tried, tested and true. Many are passed down from grandmas, aunts, great aunts, moms and the occasional kissing cousin. Others are my own twist on the original. Baking is an escape for me. I truly am happiest when I'm baking. I love sharing my baked goods and spreading the joy of baking around. Dating is not always an escape for me, but it sure is entertaining.

There were many times when I second-guessed myself while writing this book. A lot of time and energy went into it. On several occasions I thought, maybe I should focus this energy on furthering my makeup artistry career. I haven't even had a date in a couple of months because I have basically locked myself up in my condo after work to write. It didn't help watching *The Shining* one night and worrying afterward about getting cabin fever! I guess the worst I could do would be to hack up my plants.

But, whenever I had moments of doubt, a sign would occur that would make me continue on my writing journey. My first sign happened after about three straight weeks of writing. One morning, I stood in my kitchen and shouted, "Just give me a sign!" I needed to know that I should be investing so much time into this project. Later that afternoon, I was sitting at my desk writing when I heard a large rustling noise on my balcony. I looked over and there was a hawk. I said, "You must be my sign." He nodded and flew off, circling above for a few minutes. I quickly looked up the symbolism of hawks: integrity, focus, determination, strength, messenger of the Gods. Okay, sounded good to me! So, I continued, finishing my manuscript.

When the next major moment of self-doubt happened, I got another sign. I called my mother for support, and she told me that our former neighbor (from when I was five) had come by and dropped off a picture he'd found in his basement from the local newspaper. Thing was, this picture was twenty-three years old. It was from the public school fall fair. I was a pigtailed ten-year-old with my beloved (now departed) Gramps, looking at the creative writing exhibits. If that's not a sign, I don't know what is.

There were many times I felt vulnerable about putting myself out there with my stories. But then I thought, who am I kidding, because if we met you would know my whole life story in about five minutes. It's taken years of dating, many bottles of red wine and many hours of listening to Coldplay CDs to make this book possible. I've unlocked my vault of emotions. By reading it, I hope that no matter what dating stage you're at, you know you're not alone. And, you'll come away with a great sugary recipe to put a smile on your face after all the good, the bad and the fugly.

Enjoy my stories and recipes, and please feel free to make them your own.

E. B.
AKA
THE HAPPY BAKER

THE HAPPY BAKER'S
BAKING TIPS

I'm not going to get into the history of baking or chocolate or sugar.
All you need to know is that I love everything to do with baking.
If any of my recipes are low-fat, I'm sorry, it was unintentional.

- ❧ Get a cute apron; you have to look your best when trying to get over someone. ·

- ❧ I use a hammer to gently crush nuts or break up pretzels or chocolate bark…oh yeah, and it's pink. I like to coordinate my hammer with my apron.

- ❧ Get good quality ingredients, especially vanilla. My feelings aren't artificial and neither are my baking ingredients. Sometimes you can even find them at places like T.J. Maxx. But you must remain focused on the item at hand, or, if you are like me you will come out with Frye boots as well. The most expensive vanilla I ever bought, but my boots are beautiful.

- ❧ Roast your nuts. It really brings out the flavor of them. Take the extra few minutes and do this simple step. Trust me, you won't regret it.

- ❧ Keep your cookie sheets cool. I used to leave my cookie sheets on my oven when it was preheating. This causes your cookies to go flat. Nobody likes flat cookies. Also, use cooking racks. Leaving your baked goods on top of the hot oven will continue to bake them.

- ❧ Blend, blend, blend. When a recipe says light and fluffy, it means light and fluffy. You will really notice a lighter texture in your baked goods.

- ❧ That being said, when you add the dry mixture to the wet mixture, do not overstir or you will end up with heavy baked goods.

- ❧ Never underestimate the power of a sprinkle. I have an assortment of colors and shapes for every season and occasion. They really dress up a cupcake.

- ❧ You will never make icing better than your mother. I have no idea why. Mine even uses margarine. I can bake her under the table, but I can never replicate her icing.

- ❧ FYI: I use unsalted butter and large eggs for all my recipes. I love dark brown sugar, but it's really a personal preference. I use sweetened, shredded coconut as a rule.

- ❧ Store cookies and squares in an airtight container. If, for some odd reason, you have leftovers, you can freeze them…until the hot guy down the hall moves in.

- ❧ Parchment paper will be your best friend. It prevents your baked goods from sticking to your cookie sheets.

- ❧ Get to know your oven. Oven temperatures vary, so you may need to modify baking times.

- ❧ The most important baking tip: have a lot of fun. Put on the *Footloose* soundtrack, maybe the latest Madonna CD. Invite a bunch of girlfriends over to help out. Dance, sing and bake away what's-his-name.…

11

45

CHAPTER 1

THE EARLY YEARS
WHEN THE GOING GETS TOUGH, THE TOUGH GET BAKING

A look at the first kiss, first relationship, first breakup, first pair of pleather pants and first perm.

RECIPES INCLUDE:
- Me + You -You = Ice Cream Cookie Sundae
- There's a First Time for Every Cornflake Crunchie
- I Need a Drink, Irish Cream Fudge

CHAPTER 2

THEY BREAK IT, YOU BAKE IT
STORIES OF HEARTACHE AND HEARTBAKE

The relationships get harder, the baking gets better. Some recipes are more complex—serious heartbake demands it.

RECIPES INCLUDE:
- The Big Hurt Cheesecake
- You Can Kiss My Triple Decker Carrot Cake Goodbye
- Bite My Peanut Brittle, Bi-Atch

83

119

CHAPTER 3
THE GOOD, THE BAD & THE FUGLY

A POTLUCK OF DATING SHENANIGANS

From Internet dating to speed dating, dating hexes, matchmaking and the ever popular computer breakup. Yep, I've survived 'em all.

RECIPES INCLUDE:

· Speed-Dating Quickies

· My Friends Think I'm Cursed White Chocolate Bark

· I'm Not Dutch, Apple Crisp

CHAPTER 4
SINGLE & SASSY

NOW WHAT?!?!

What's a girl supposed to do?
Let my stories and recipes help you through it.

Sure we might be single and sassy, but we are just waiting for someone to sweep us off our independent, well-dressed feet!

RECIPES INCLUDE:

· My Eggs Aren't Getting Any Younger Crème Brûlée

· No Money, No Honey, Butter Tarts

· Where Have All the Good Cowboys Gone Cookie?

WHEN THE GOING GETS

TOUGH

CHAPTER 1

THE EARLY YEARS

THE TOUGH GET

BAKING

I NEED A DRINK, IRISH CREAM FUDGE

MY mom prescribes Irish cream for almost everything, including men!!

3 cups semisweet chocolate chips
1 cup white chocolate chips
¼ cup butter

3 cups confectioners' sugar
1 cup Irish cream liqueur

1½ cups flaked filberts (hazelnuts), roasted at 325°F (160°C) for 5–7 minutes.

- Melt chocolate and butter in a medium saucepan over low heat.

- Remove from heat, stir in confectioners' sugar and Irish cream until the mixture is smooth.

- Stir in nuts. Put mixture in a greased 8-inch-square pan, spread evenly.

- Refrigerate until firm. Cut into small pieces.

- Please do not eat and drive; this fudge has some serious punch.

HIGH SCHOOL
PASS
HEARTACHE

MY FIRST CRUSH

It was 1979. I was attending the first day of kindergarten back home in my little village of 900 people (middle of nowhere, Ontario, Canada). With my Pebbles Flintstone necklace around my neck, the perfect complement to my brand-new red-and-blue gingham dress, I was set. I prepared myself for anything this "school" thing could possibly throw my way…except him! He was a farm kid, with dark hair, brown eyes and lips that would make Angelina Jolie jealous. Wow, they didn't teach me how to deal with HIM on *Sesame Street*. "Ouvre la fenetre" didn't cut it. As I opened the classroom window to wave goodbye to my mother, I pondered if I should attempt to slip out and avoid the serious heartache I knew I was in for.

From that day on, and all through public school, my infatuation persisted. One by one, year after year, I convinced my friends to ask my crush out while I nervously hid. But to my dismay, he always said no. I mean, who would want to date a freckle-faced kid with a red Afro and glasses the size of her mother's 1980 Chrysler Cordoba? I knew I wasn't textbook cute (although my mother tried to convince me otherwise). I liked being different; it just came natural for me. But no matter how hurt and small I felt over the rejection, I never felt like giving up or changing my style. And with Aries as my fiery competitive moon sign, I wasn't going to stop crushing on him without a fight.

I was a very athletic kid, so my crush and I were on the same baseball team throughout most of public school. When it came time for the annual baseball team picture in fourth grade, I was ready to make a serious impression on this guy. Wait 'til he saw me all dolled up for the photo! There was no way he would not want to be my boyfriend after that. I freshened up my Afro perm, cleaned my glasses with a squeegee, and pulled on my "Thriller" pleather pants. (Nothing says baseball like a pair of pleather pants.) So, after a few hours of primping my new look I was ready to make my debut on the baseball field.

All the boys teased me (including my crush) that I looked like Annie…ANNIE!! Would Annie have worn a pair of pleather pants to baseball? I think not! I guess the look was better suited for "MJ" and his world tour, not for "EB" and her baseball photo. Crushed and hurt, I walked home with my baseball glove on my head hiding my beloved fro. My mother came out to greet me. She could hear me crying all the way down the street. She tried to comfort me and promised to buy me a red pleather "Thriller" jacket to make me feel better. I felt like giving up. I was so disappointed. Maybe I should dye my hair blond… grow out the perm. Maybe being different wasn't that great, if all you felt was awkward and humiliated. Maybe I could see without my glasses. "For the love of God, would somebody design a pair that didn't take up half of my face!"

After a cold refreshing glass of purple Kool-Aid, I thought, I have got to pull myself together. I was not giving up on my crush. It was gonna happen. So what if he teased me and made me feel the size of a gnat? It was only because he actually liked me, right? I bounced back quickly from the teasing and tapped back into my competitive spirit.

In a small Canadian town, every kid generally figure skates or plays hockey. Back when I was a kid, girls didn't play hockey, so I was a figure skater and a pretty darn good one at that. I was about eleven by season's end, when it was time to show off all my progress to my friends and family by creating a skating solo. I knew my crush and his family would be there. What could I do to get his attention this time and get him to know I was a cool chick? Since the pleather pants had failed miserably, I needed something a little more his style. When I announced to my figure skating coach I would do my year-end solo to "D.T." by AC/DC, she just shook her head. It was his favorite band; how could he not like me after that?

It had been some time since the baseball incident. A couple years wiser, I felt confident and ready to give it another shot. My fro had grown out and was neatly put up in a French braid. My mother had sewn the most beautiful turquoise dress for me, which I had designed and was not short on ruffles and bows. I also had the attitude to match. The arena lights dimmed, the spotlight situated on me, the music cued. I skated like I never had before. I felt as light as a feather. My twists, jumps, turns and choreography were perfect. I officially rocked out my solo. I smiled with satisfaction as I heard the applause. But guess who wasn't clapping or even paying any attention? My Crush! I thought, "Hello, McFly, awesome girl down here, skating her tushy off for you!! What do I have to do? Pleather didn't work, AC/DC didn't work. Do I have to buy you a John Deere tractor to make you like me?" I couldn't afford that. I had spent most of my money on jelly shoes and hair straightener!

Most people would have given up by that point. Maybe I would have if he hadn't been the only cute guy within a 50-mile radius. Though I still did continue to crush on my guy all through my teens, I had become a lot prettier by standard terms. Long gone were the days of giant glasses and perms. My long red hair was the envy of most people. Not to mention the great physique I'd acquired from figure skating. And, I continued to go out of my way to be near him. I went so far as to spend an afternoon farming with him, driving around in a tractor. Considering I was highly allergic to hay and practically everything else outdoors, this wasn't the best choice. Oh, the things we did for hot farm guys.

Fast-forward to my nineteenth B-day, a big deal up here in Canada. Woo-hoo, I was finally a legally drinking adult. No more sneaking peach schnapps out of my mother's liquor cabinet. I could legitimately drink the good stuff. Maybe Baby Duck. Maybe Coors Light. The choices were endless. I'd been living in Toronto, a big city a couple hours away, for the past year taking a cosmetics program at college. But, I had decided I needed to go home and celebrate my B-day country style. Nothing says, "I'm an adult now" like a good old-fashioned beer tent!!

It had been a year since I'd seen my crush. I was now more mature, wiser and drunker than I had ever been. As I sat down at a picnic table with my friends and family, I noticed my crush at the other end of the beer tent. HAPPY BIRTHDAY to me!! The stars must have been aligned that night because before I knew it we were making out on my grandparents' back lawn (sorry, Grandma). I was really trying to enjoy the moment. I had finally made it happen. All the years of his failure to recognize me as a prime candidate for a girlfriend disappeared in our first smooch. I felt like life was just a little bit sweeter. I felt like if I could do this I could do anything. Canada's first female prime minister, here I come! The moment could not have been more perfect. It seemed like a dream…until I heard my auntie calling me. OMG, Auntie, do not ruin this moment for me! I can disown you, you know. Thankfully, she got the hint and left us alone. It's not like we were doing anything bad. Just a little kissing. And that's all I needed. I didn't need a relationship. After all those years, I just needed to know my crush liked me enough to make out with me. Okay, so it took fifteen years and a few beers, but it still happened. Thank goodness for my Aries moon sign!

SLOW AND STEADY WINS THE,
PEANUT BUTTER CUPCAKES

FOOLS DON'T RUSH BAKING.

2	cups all-purpose flour
2	cups sugar
½	cup cocoa
2	tsps. baking soda
1	tsp. baking powder
½	tsp. salt
1	cup oil
1	cup milk
2	eggs, slightly beaten
1	tsp. vanilla extract
1	cup hot water

ICING

½	cup butter, softened
1	cup peanut butter
3	tbsp. hot water
2	cups confectioners' sugar

✪ Preheat oven to 350°F (175°C).

✪ Line cupcake tins; makes 18 cupcakes.

✪ In a large bowl, sift together dry ingredients.

✪ Add oil, milk, vanilla, beaten eggs; blend well. Stir in hot water; mix well.

✪ Fill lined cupcake tins. Bake for 22–25 minutes. Let cool.

✪ FOR ICING: Blend together butter and peanut butter until light and fluffy. Gradually add confectioners' sugar and hot water (alternating) until desired texture is achieved.

✪ Ice cupcakes and enjoy!

½	cup sugar
¼	cup brown sugar, packed
½	cup butter, softened
1	tsp. vanilla extract
1	egg
1	cup all-purpose flour
1	cup quick-cooking oats
1	tsp. baking soda
½	tsp. salt
¾	cup semisweet chocolate chips
½	cup coconut

Vanilla ice cream
Caramel sauce

- Preheat oven to 375°F (190°C).

- In a large bowl, blend together sugars and butter until light and fluffy; add egg and vanilla.

- Stir in flour, oats, baking soda and salt; mix well.

- Stir in chocolate chips and coconut.

- Drop by tablespoonfuls onto a lined cookie sheet.

- Bake for 7–9 minutes until golden brown.

- Remove cookies from oven.

- While the cookies are still warm, place them on top of a generous scoop of ice cream.

- Drizzle caramel sauce all over cookies and ice cream.

MY FIRST KISS

The Big Event, I remember it well.

My best bud, Nikki Rae, and I were at a teen dance at the local arena. We were all of fifteen years old. We entered the dance not knowing what the evening had in store, as innocent as can be. I had a gut feeling that night would be different than any other dance.

Across the crowded room of Santana skinny jeans and acid-washed denim jackets, we spied them. "Well now, those guys are kinda cute," we said to each other AND they were not locals…bonus. Nikki Rae took dibs on the darker-haired mullet guy. Billy Ray Cyrus had nothing on this one. His fitted jeans showed off his cute derrière.

My guy was medium built, sandy-blond hair, no mullet. They, of course, liked our fashion sense, too. At least they'd better. It had taken me two hours to carefully put safety pins up the side of my jeans. Nikki Rae was rocking her trusty leather vest. It never failed to impress. After a few rounds of flirty glances, they finally made the move and asked us to dance. Cool. Slow dancing to rock ballads, I was an old hat at that. As we swayed back and forth, arms extended straight out, I started wondering what it would be like to kiss those cherry Chapstick–moistened lips. It was time to see what I'd been missing out on that so many of my friends had known for at least a year by now. I knew I was a late bloomer; I was just a little picky, and the moment had to be right.

After a few slow dances and some ice-cold sodas, they asked if we wanted to go outside to "talk." I wasn't born yesterday, buddy. I know what *talk* means, and I was as ready as ever.

Every year my pals and I would get together at the Lions Park to talk about the boys we had kissed. We would hang out on the swings and talk about our love-life adventures. When it came to my turn, we just skipped by. That year it would change! My story would be the envy of all my friends.

In the parking lot, Nikki Rae and I with our new BFs Mullet Boy and Blondie just stared at each other because nobody dared to make a move. Somebody had better say something because the night wasn't getting any warmer, or less awkward. We didn't want to let the boys know how silly we felt. We had to be mature fifteen-year-olds! Finally, my guy suggested we get "more comfortable" and go relax in the backseat of his beautiful blue Chevette. Obviously, he didn't notice how tight my jeans were. If sitting down in the tightest jeans in the world as they cut off your circulation was comfortable, well then so be it. My best bud and Mullet Boy headed off to a nearby, dimly lit park bench.

Meanwhile in the Chevette, Blondie and I nervously chatted about who knows what, probably the weather. That's what we countryfolk love to talk about. I knew he wanted to make a move, and I wanted it to happen. I knew that was The Moment that would change my life. Just like in the movies. Maybe I would hear angels singing? Maybe we would ride off into the sunset together? Goodbye Joey McIntyre and New Kids on the Block (NKOTB); I was moving on.

He moved closer and then so close I could smell his Juicy Fruit gum. I was only seconds away from that magic moment. Until I accidentally poked him in his eye with my teased, hairsprayed bangs. Wow, my mom wasn't lying when she said my hair was like a weapon. He sucked it up and dealt with it. Kissing me was definitely more important than tending to his injury. He went in for The Kiss.

"This is interesting," I thought. Rain? The forecast hadn't called for rain. Nope, not rain—saliva, and a lot of it. I wished my face were made of superabsorbent paper towel. I'd waited fifteen years for this!! "I'll go back to kissing my pillow, thank you. Please tell me it gets better. My Joey McIntyre poster kisses better than you." I could think of a million other things I would rather do with my mouth, like eating chocolate, even unsweetened baking chocolate. Blondie asked if it was okay. I said, "Yes, the best kiss I've ever had." It wasn't a lie.

Even though the kissing was pretty bad, I continued to date my guy for a couple of weeks. Why? Because blood is thicker than water, and my best friend Nikki Rae really liked his best friend Mullet Boy. I couldn't let her down. So if making out with Hoover Dam was what I had to do for best friends to stay together, then so be it.

We were like Cagney & Lacey, Laverne & Shirley. Hmm...maybe we were more like Beavis & Butthead. We soon realized that neither one of us liked the guys. We were both taking one for the team, just so we could still hang out. Since best friends think alike, we both thought the kissing thing was highly overrated, and we should always, always carry paper towel in our back pocket.

To this day we are still best buds. I avoid blue cars at all costs. And yes, the kissing thing has greatly improved. Thank goodness, because I can't find my Joey McIntyre poster anywhere!

The Adventures of Erin & Nikki Rae

THERE IS A FIRST TIME FOR EVERYTHING.
DO YOU REMEMBER YOUR FIRST KISS?

½ **cup brown sugar, packed**
½ **cup dark corn syrup**
½ **cup smooth peanut butter**

1 **tsp. vanilla extract**

½ **cup peanuts**
3 **cups cornflakes**

- ✪ In a medium saucepan over medium heat, bring the sugar, corn syrup and peanut butter to a boil until the texture resembles sticky toffee.

- ✪ Remove from heat; stir in vanilla. Stir in peanuts and cornflakes until evenly coated.

- ✪ Drop by tablespoonfuls onto a lined cookie sheet. Let cool in fridge. Store in an airtight container.

PEANUT BUTTER CRISPY CUPS

WHAT can I say?
I HaVe TO DO THINGS aT MY OWN Pace.

1	10.5 oz. milk chocolate bar, chopped into medium-sized pieces
1	cup peanut butter chips
2	cups crisped rice
24	mini cupcake liners

⚹ Line mini cupcake trays.

⚹ Over low heat in a medium saucepan, melt chocolate and peanut butter chips.

⚹ Stir in crisped rice, until evenly coated. Fill mini cupcake trays; let set.

High School
Sweetheart

1¼   cups all-purpose flour
¼   tsp. baking soda
¼   tsp. salt

½   cup butter, softened
½   cup sugar
½   cup brown sugar

Juice of 1 lemon, remove seeds
1   egg
1   tsp. vanilla extract

Coconut to roll dough in.

YOU ARE NOT AS
SWEET
AS MY
SUGAR COOKIES

- Preheat oven to 350°F (175°C).

- Sift together the flour, baking soda and salt; set aside.

- In a medium mixing bowl, cream together the butter and sugars.

- Mix in lemon juice, egg and vanilla.

- Add dry ingredients. Wrap dough in plastic and put in the refrigerator until easy to handle.

- Roll dough into 1-inch balls and then roll in coconut. Place balls on a lined cookie sheet and flatten with your fingers.

- Bake for 12–15 minutes, until slightly golden. Let cool on wire cooling racks.

LATE BLOOMER

You didn't have to tell me I was one, I knew it. Even after my first kiss, it was a while until I had another. Since the kissing incident was not a good one in my books, I had reverted back to daydreaming about Joey McIntyre. But I did still think about having a boyfriend. Why not? All my friends were doing it. Maybe I just needed to see what I was missing.

So as my love for Joey faded and reality set in, I started noticing some cute boys in my high school. I had grown out of the pop-music phase and into the '80s hair-band phase. Yep, I was comfortable dating a guy who had hair just as long and luxurious as my own. Most of the boys I went for were, of course, the bad-boy rocker type who didn't really have girlfriends but managed to break many hearts.

I never really went on dates, unless you called making out in a cornfield at a field party a date. But the following year when my girlfriends and I got together at the swings at Lions Park, I'd definitely made up for some lost time. I had kissed a handful of boys by then, none of whom had become my boyfriend. I didn't mind that, though. I had a lot of fun and very little heartache and a new fondness for cornfields. Sure, I didn't get to stick my hand in the back pocket of my boyfriend's jeans while parading around the halls of high school. I'd even gone to prom with a friend because we were the only single people left. My friends were always having so much drama with boys and I was happily avoiding all of that, until I dated the "baddest" boy of them all.

He was the closest I came to having a boyfriend in high school. It was at the very end of my last year. He was a few years older than me and in college. I knew he was a little unruly. My instincts told me *no*, but his pretty green eyes said *yes*.

I remembered Green Eyes well from high school. He was a super-cute rocker with gorgeous honey-colored hair. He would tour around town in his souped-up red and white Firebird. I knew he liked me all during high school, but I was nervous. He was older, and was constantly getting into trouble, so I would always brush off his advances. Since I was inexperienced with relationships and boys, I'd felt really intimidated by him. This guy was the dude of all dudes. I thought Green Eyes was so persistent, and he seemed much sweeter than his reputation made him out to be. Maybe I would give him a chance. So, I did. He kept saying he felt like he was in a dream. He couldn't believe we were actually dating. I thought this guy wasn't bad at all; he was a sweetheart. Well, apparently the chase was much better than the catch because about a month after he caught me, he seemed a little less than interested. But of course by that time I was hooked on him and needed the devoted attention he'd always used to give me. Who cares if he could have easily passed for a Whitesnake roadie? That guy was meant to be my boyfriend.

I wasn't sure what had changed to make him not into me anymore. Maybe he wasn't used to girls that wore chastity belts. It wasn't really a belt—more like a sash. Anyway, I knew I didn't fit whatever image he'd had in his head of me before we hooked up.

Our courtship ended when I surprised him at his college apartment in the city about an hour away. Problem was, his city girlfriend had decided to surprise him, too. I caught them making out on his back porch. There wasn't enough room in his bachelor apartment for all of us, and there certainly wasn't enough hairspray for the three of us to share. His city girlfriend decided to leave after she knew I wasn't going anywhere. I was in complete shock and unable to drive safely. So, uncomfortably, I had to stay over without speaking a word to him. It's hard to speak when your jaw is on the floor.

I left for high school in the morning, only asking him for my high school photo back. I had given him the biggest size, and you know those things weren't cheap. He wasn't worthy of it. My first class was Shop. Just me and a roomful of guys, boys, evil spawn. The teacher better keep me away from the nail gun, or it won't be pretty. Of course, when I came home from school, my mother had the "I told you so" look on her face. She greatly disapproved of this relationship, but I was stubborn and had disobeyed her anyway.

I did run into Green Eyes at a field party not long after that. He thought it would be funny to tease me in front of his friends about our breakup. Of course, it was not funny and I continued to pick up my jaw from the ground. Well, at least I ended high school with a bang. That short-lived relationship made up for all the drama I had missed out on. I will give him some credit, though, because about a year or so after the incident we ran into each other at a local bar, The Rubberboot. He came up to me with sympathetic green eyes and apologized for the way he'd treated me and walked away. I've never seen him again.

THREE'S A CROWD, ROCKY ROAD BARS

IT'S A ROCKY ROAD BUT SOMEBODY HAS TO BAKE IT.

½ cup butter, softened
⅓ cup sugar
1 cup all-purpose flour

1¼ cups mini marshmallows
1 cup semisweet chocolate chips
1 cup walnuts, lightly crushed

- Preheat oven to 350°F (175°C), grease an 8-inch-square pan.
- Beat butter and sugar until light and fluffy.
- Stir in flour and ½ cup of the walnuts. Press into prepared pan. Bake for 15–18 minutes.
- Remove from oven. Sprinkle chocolate chips, marshmallows and remaining nuts over base. Return to oven and bake for 5–7 minutes until marshmallows are slightly puffed.
- Remove from oven and with the tip of a knife gently swirl the chocolate.
- Let cool and enjoy!

½	cup brown sugar, packed
¾	cup sugar
¾	cup butter, softened
2	eggs
1	tsp. vanilla extract
2¼	cups all-purpose flour
1½	tsps. baking powder
¼	tsp. salt
¾	cup dried cranberries
5	squares (1 ounce/square) white baking chocolate, coarsely chopped
1	square white chocolate

- Preheat oven to 350°F (175°C), grease an 8-inch-square pan.

- In a medium-sized bowl, blend together the sugars and butter until light and fluffy.

- Add eggs and vanilla.

- In a separate bowl, sift together flour, baking powder and salt; add to wet mixture. Mix until just combined.

- Stir in cranberries and five squares of chopped chocolate. Press into prepared pan and bake for 35–40 minutes. Remove from oven.

- Melt remaining square of white chocolate and drizzle on top of bars. Let cool and cut.

NO PAIN NO GAIN, OATMEAL RAISIN COOKIE

YOU HAVE TO START SOMEWHERE EVEN IF IT'S A CORNFIELD.

¾ **cup brown sugar, packed**
½ **cup sugar**
¾ **cup butter, softened**

2 **eggs**
1 **tsp. vanilla extract**

1½ **cups all-purpose flour**
1 **tsp. baking soda**
½ **tsp. salt**
½ **tsp. cinnamon**

2 **cups quick-cooking oats**
1 **cup raisins**

- Preheat oven to 375°F (190°C).

- In a medium-sized bowl, blend together sugars and butter until light and fluffy.

- Add eggs and vanilla; mix thoroughly.

- In a separate bowl, sift together flour, baking soda, salt and cinnamon; stir into wet mixture. Add oats and raisins; stir until mixed.

- Drop by heaping tablespoonfuls, two inches apart, onto lined cookie sheet. Bake for 10–12 minutes.

FRIENDSHIP BREAD LASTS FOREVER

THIS RECIPE TAKES LONGER TO MAKE THAN MOST OF MY RELATIONSHIPS HAVE LASTED, BUT THE OUTCOME IS MUCH BETTER.

FOR THE STARTER:

1	packet active dry yeast (2¼ tsps.)
¼	cup warm water
3	cups sugar, separated
3	cups all-purpose flour, separated
3	cups warm milk, separated

FOR THE FRIENDSHIP BREAD:

2	cups all-purpose flour
1	package instant vanilla pudding mix
1¼	tsps. baking powder
1	tsp. ground cinnamon
½	tsp. salt
½	tsp. baking soda
1	cup starter
1	cup sugar
⅔	cup vegetable oil
¼	cup milk
3	eggs
1	tsp. vanilla extract

TO MAKE STARTER:

1. Dissolve yeast in warm water. Stir together (using a non-metallic spoon) 1 cup sugar, 1 cup flour and 1 cup milk in a non-metallic bowl or container. Add yeast mixture and stir. Cover, leave at room temperature.

2. Day 1: Do nothing; it has been stirred.

3. Days 2, 3 and 4: Stir.

4. Day 5: Add 1 cup milk, 1 cup sugar, 1 cup flour.

5. Days: 6, 7, 8 and 9: Stir.

6. Day 10: Add 1 cup milk, 1 cup sugar, 1 cup flour and stir. Remove 1 cup to make your first bread; give 3 cups to friends along with the above directions, starting with Day 2, and the recipe for friendship bread.

7. You can either start the 10-day process again (starting at Step 2) or make your friendship bread from your 1-cup starter. You can also freeze the starter in 1-cup measures for later use. Frozen starter will take at least 3 hours at room temperature to thaw before using.

TO MAKE FRIENDSHIP BREAD:

- Preheat oven to 350°F (175°C).

- Sift together in a medium bowl the flour, pudding mix, baking powder, cinnamon, salt and baking soda; set aside.

- In large mixing bowl combine friendship starter, oil, eggs, milk, vanilla and sugar; mix well.

- Stir the flour mixture into the wet mixture; mixing until just combined; do not overmix. Pour into two 9 x 5 x 3-inch loaf pans. Bake at 350°F (175°C) for 50–60 minutes.

- Feel free to add ½ cup of your favorite nuts to the bread and sprinkle with brown sugar.

FOR THE LOVE OF
TOFFEE CRACKER GOODNESS

1   **package saltine crackers (app. 35 crackers)**

1   **cup brown sugar, packed**
1   **cup butter**

2   **cups semisweet chocolate chips**
½   **cup slivered almonds, roasted at 325˚F (160˚C) degrees for 5–7 minutes.**

- Preheat oven to 400˚F (200˚C).

- Place crackers side by side on a lined cookie sheet with edges.

- In a saucepan, bring brown sugar and butter to a boil. Continue boiling for 3 minutes; stirring constantly.

- Pour evenly over saltine crackers.

- Bake for 5 minutes. Remove from oven and pour chocolate chips and almonds over crackers. Let sit a couple minutes until chocolate chips are softened, then spread evenly.

- Cool and break into pieces.

A+
Broken Heart Test

THE BIG ONE. Pt. I

After I got over dating all my long-haired rocker types, I had my first *real* relationship. I was almost twenty-two! Long gone were the days of my guy-stealing black eyeliner and hairspray from my makeup bag. Like they always say, it happened when I least expected it.

I had sworn off men for about a year. I was tired of meeting guys, getting to know them, and then either he or I would run the other way. Obviously I wasn't ready for a committed relationship, so why try to force it. I hated feeling like I was a failure at relationships or just being disappointed that another one didn't work out. So to avoid that feeling, I decided to focus on myself, my own interests and my career.

I signed up for baseball on a co-ed team and was more concerned with scoring runs than scoring dates. BUT, there was one guy on the team who stood out. At first I thought he was a lawyer coming to give me papers from an inheritance. Then I realized, not a lawyer but a fellow baseball player. He was a sharp dresser, friendly, mature and very proper. The "baddest" thing this guy did was jaywalk. His friends laughed when I thought we were around the same age. Apparently he was five years older than me, but you couldn't tell by looking at him. Even though he was older, he was so easy to talk to, and we quickly became friends. That's all I wanted. I didn't *need* to date him. Dating wasn't even in my vocabulary at that point.

To my surprise he phoned after a couple of ball games to make sure I was coming to the next one. Of course, I said, I wouldn't miss it for the world. Why was this guy calling to make sure I'm coming? It's not like he's in charge of attendance for the team. My roommate thought he had a crush on me. "Yeah right," I said, he's just being friendly.

Hmm…maybe he did like me? Without being fully aware, I was starting to crush on him, too. I didn't realize this until I saw him at the next game when I instantly got butterflies in my stomach. At first I thought maybe the feeling was anxiety over the fact our team was last in the league. Nope, not anxiety. That feeling wasn't going anywhere. The whole game I felt completely distracted by him. So, I focused my attention on getting to know him better. Those moments of attraction are funny where everything is in slow motion. You zone everything and everyone out, except for him. We were slowly falling for each other. It was a pace I liked, because anything faster would have sent him to the dugout.

The next game, I thought, "I'm going to look super cute; it's time to pull out my most fitted pair of baseball shorts. Maybe I will get to first base in more ways than one." Then when I was leaving my underground parking spot, I accidentally ripped my bumper off my beautiful 1986 Delta 88. Don't even ask me how that happened. Maybe it's because the parking spots in these city condos can't handle a luxury-sized car. I just thought this guy was going to think, "Couldn't she have come up with a better excuse if she doesn't want to see me than 'I ripped my bumper off my car?'" Being the handy girl I am, I tied it back on with rope, but I was too late to make the game.

As expected, he gave me a call after the game to see why I didn't show up. He didn't think I was crazy after I told him why, and then he asked me out on a date. Holy Moly, a date, an actual date! I quickly called my mother, and to this day she remembers how excited I was when I told her I'd been asked out on a proper date, no more cornfields for me. Maybe I *should* give this dating thing another shot. Different guy, different relationship—surely I can't repeat my same pattern with every guy I meet. Maybe he will be "The One." Considering I am a hopeless romantic and, of course, with my competitive Aries moon sign, I had to give it a shot or I would always wonder, "What If?"

Considering the age difference, I knew this was not going to be the "Let's hang out and listen to my new CD" kind of date or "Hey, let's make out in this bar" kind of date. This would be a real date: eating food, having conversation. A date like that required a new outfit and a new attitude. I'm not going to let my past discourage me. This girl's moving up in her dating life. I'm gonna make my momma proud!

Since I was the car owner in this duo, I picked him up in my Delta 88. No problem. I'm not embarrassed to drive a car the size of a small island. I'm sure it's not the first time the man has seen one, maybe with someone fifty years older than me, but nonetheless I'm sure he has. Dinner was at a "fancy" place, no plastic cutlery here. You can't even pump gas outside this restaurant. I thought, "I can get used to this mature style of dating." So we continued going on plastic cutlery–free dates about twice a week, then three times and so on....

Now, since I did have that habit of dating guys for a couple of weeks, getting freaked out about commitment, then running the other way, I was expecting the same pattern to happen. But it didn't. Two weeks passed, then two months. Slowly but surely I was figuring out this relationship thing. After the two months came and went with The Big One I started thinking this was going to be the relationship I was hoping for. My first real committed relationship; I should get a medal for that. I've seen one too many unhappy relationships in my life, and I was hell-bent and determined not to let that happen to me. Usually I'd get out of Dodge early on, but this relationship was one that I didn't need or want to run away from. I guess I was just happy to finally feel like I could go the distance with someone.

Even though we were very different, we were still a good match. He collected baseball cards, I collected *Metal Edge* magazines. His casual clothes were khakis; mine were ripped-up jogging pants. It's hard to explain; I guess I was content to finally find a man that I felt at ease with. I guess we had enough in common to make it work: conversations, movies, dinners. I was also excited about trying new things The Big One was into, like art galleries and traveling. I felt so proper. Don't get me wrong, our differences almost cost us our relationship in the beginning. Being the country girl I am, it didn't faze me to go to the loo behind a bush at a city park (it was dark out, of course). That did not fly with The Big One. He was so embarrassed he stopped talking to me for the remainder of the evening. First of all, it was my birthday; second, I'd had lots of liquids and third, there was no dang washroom for at least as far as my drunken eyes could see. My roomie was also with me celebrating my B-day, and encouraged me to go behind a bush rather than in my pants! So I did. Apparently The Big One and I did not take the same etiquette class growing up. I guess I needed to refine my country ways to mesh with this proper city slicker. It was something I wasn't used to doing, but that's okay.

There we were, The Big One and I, getting along pleasantly. We got past the "Do I call him/her my boyfriend/girlfriend in public?" thing. I should get a medal for that, too. Things couldn't have been better. I felt loved, happy and safe with him. I never felt like I could get really hurt by The Big One.

Until it happened. We ran into the first big relationship bump. It's like a fist in the stomach when that happens, like your world is ending. I did not think twice about inviting him home for the holidays. The Big One apparently did. He felt that he wasn't ready to bring home the love of his life to meet his entire family. What, am I not good enough for your family? Are you embarrassed to have a hot, awesome girlfriend? I felt so hurt, and all the protective walls I had let down were being built back up. After a big fight and one day of not speaking, we got over it. I still felt wary about letting my heart be so open, but then I realized guys are just different and they generally make a bigger deal out of things. Okay, where are we—three medals by now? Christmas, here we come…the happy, merry, committed couple. Extra turkey for me, hold the cranberry sauce.

Years passed, after many holidays and celebrations, everything was going smoothly. Until our next major roadblock. My beloved roomie of five years was moving out. A fellow country girl, she'd had enough of the city and needed to move back to the boonies. I didn't want to get another roommate. The Big One and I had been dating for more than three years now. I thought that was more than enough time to know if you are ready to take your relationship to "the next level." I was ready. Apparently again, he was not. "Dude, we are not getting hitched, just shacking up. What's the big deal? If you don't want to, then I will just find someone else who will." The Big One talked it over with his buddies. They let him know it wasn't as much of a deal as he was making it out to be. If it didn't work out, we would just break up and move out. So we moved in. Next medal.

Things were amazing. The Big One realized living together was great for our relationship. He was buying me flowers, making fabulous French dinners (hence my love of French desserts). I gained the happy five, ten, probably twenty pounds when all was said and done. We would travel; it was fun even though he made more of an itinerary on our trips than the most demanding trip organizer. I ended up in a hospital at the end of our European vacation, because I was so run down my entire body was swollen and covered in hives. Thank goodness it happened in Amsterdam; those guys have the right medicine there to fix just about anything.

So, The Big One and I survived moving in with each other, and we realized it was great for our relationship. I know I needed it. The last thing I wanted was to feel bitter that everyone around us had relationships that were doing great and making steady progress. I was just glad ours was finally making some progress, too. Slow and steady, I knew it took longer than most of our friends, but luckily for The Big One I was a patient and persistent woman.

Two happy, slightly more plump people, enjoying a fulfilling relationship. That, of course, would eventually lead to marriage, children and a lifetime of happiness. To be continued.

JUMBO BANANA PANCAKES FOR TWO

Remember when sharing was fun?

1   cup all-purpose flour
1   tbsp. sugar
2   tsps. baking powder
½   tsp. cinnamon
¼   tsp. nutmeg
¼   tsp. salt

1   egg, beaten
1   cup milk
2   tbsps. vegetable oil
2   very ripe bananas, mashed

Real maple syrup

* Sift together all dry ingredients.

* In another bowl, combine egg, milk, oil and mashed bananas.

* Stir dry mixture into banana mixture until just combined; mixture will be a little lumpy.

* Warm frying pan over medium-low heat. Measure 1 cup batter; cook on both sides until golden brown. Serve with real maple syrup.

GATEAU AU CHOCOLATE

PARLEZ VOUS FRANCAIS?
NOPE, NEITHER DO I.
BUT I DO SPEAK THE
UNIVERSAL LANGUAGE
OF BAKING.

¾	cup sugar (set aside 3 tbsp.)
8	ozs. 70% dark chocolate, cut into small chunks
4	ozs. milk chocolate, cut into small chunks
¾	cup butter, cut into small pieces
2	tsps. vanilla extract
5	eggs, separated
¼	cup all-purpose flour
½	tsp. salt

Confectioners' sugar for dusting

- ✪ Preheat oven to 325°F (160°C).

- ✪ Cut out a piece of parchment paper to fit the bottom of a 9-inch springform pan. Butter the pan and sprinkle evenly with sugar.

- ✪ In a medium saucepan over low heat, combine the chocolate, butter and sugar until melted and sugar is dissolved.

- ✪ Remove the pan from heat, stir in the vanilla and let the mixture cool a little.

- ✪ Beat the egg yolks into the mixture; stir in flour.

- ✪ In a super-clean bowl beat the egg whites slowly until they are frothy. Add the salt and increase the speed until soft peaks form. Add 3 tbsps. of sugar, continue beating until stiff and glossy.

- ✪ Beat ⅓ of the egg whites into the chocolate mixture; then fold in the rest of the egg whites.

- ✪ Pour the batter into the prepared pan. Gently tap to release any air bubbles.

- ✪ Bake for 30–35 minutes until the top springs back when you lightly touch it.

- ✪ Let cool. Sprinkle with confectioners' sugar.

I FINALLY FOUND A KEEPER,
GOURMET CARAMEL APPLES

MAKE THESE AND HE'S SURE TO STICK AROUND.
THAT IS, IF YOU WANT HIM TO.

20	individually wrapped caramels, unwrapped
1½	tbsps. water
2	large apples
2	sticks
½	cup 70% dark chocolate, chopped
¼	tsp. cinnamon
¼	cup almond slivers, roast at 325°F (160°C) for 3–5 min.

⊛ Melt caramels and water in a small saucepan over medium-low heat, stirring often. Insert sticks into the tops of the apples. Evenly spoon melted caramel over apples. Let set on a plate lined with parchment paper; refrigerate.

⊛ Meanwhile over low heat, melt chocolate in a small saucepan. Stir in cinnamon; mix thoroughly.

⊛ Dip tops of apples in the melted dark chocolate, then dip tops in the almonds. Drizzle the remaining chocolate over the apples.

⊛ A caramel apple a day will not keep the dentist away; these are very serious apples. Brush carefully after.

WANTED

THE CUPCAKE DUO

★★ REWARD ★★
SPEEDY BREAK-UP RECOVERY

STORIES OF HEARTACHE

CHAPTER 2
THEY BREAK IT, YOU BAKE IT

AND HEARTBAKE

ALMOST PARADISE BREAD

WELL, AT LEAST THE BREAD IS PARADISE.

2	cups all-purpose flour
½	tsp. salt
1	tsp. baking soda
½	tsp. baking powder
1	cup sugar
1	tsp. cinnamon
2	large ripe bananas, mashed
4	small slices of canned mango, cut into small pieces
½	cup crushed pineapple, drained
½	cup vegetable oil
2	eggs, beaten
1	tsp. vanilla extract
¾	cup coconut

- Preheat oven to 350°F (175°C).

- In a large mixing bowl, sift the flour, salt, baking soda, baking powder, sugar and cinnamon.

- In a medium bowl, combine the banana, mango, pineapple, oil, eggs and vanilla. Add to flour mixture; stir until just blended. Stir in coconut.

- Pour batter in a greased loaf pan. Bake for 60 minutes or until a toothpick inserted in the center comes out clean.

THE BIG ONE. PT. II

At this part of the relationship, there are fewer medals given out. Some may even be taken away. But don't worry. I still came out a lot wiser and a winner.

After three years of living together, we'd just become too comfortable. The Big One was no longer interested in me, at least not the way I needed him to be. I'd tried everything. I would participate in things The Big One liked just so we could spend time together. Off we went to driving ranges, museums, vacations where we'd always have to "learn" something. Okay. So, I know not everyone likes going to country music concerts and visiting small towns, but at least you should do it for your woman! She did it for you. Any conversation I would bring up about marriage or kids was answered with "maybe someday." That answer was fine with me for a few years because I kept hoping one day he would change his mind. Then I started resenting him for saying it, so I stopped asking. I guess he was thinking "Why buy the cow when the milk is free?" Well, this cow was thinking about greener pastures, buddy, if you didn't change your mind.

I stopped participating in his activities. I visited my family on my own because I knew he didn't like being out of the city. Basically, the only activities we did together were going to the movies and going out for dinner. I think I would have that in common with Genghis Khan. So, my relationship with The Big One was steadily going downhill. Especially when he started a more committed relationship with someone else...cable TV. It even got to the point where if I spoke to him, he would just point to the TV, as if to say, "I'm too busy watching this show on fishing right now to have a conversation with you." I like to think I was more important than fishing lures. Apparently, he was too busy pointing to realize he was still in a relationship with a woman who had one foot out the door.

One problem I have to this day is being nonconfrontational. So, instead of talking about what is driving me crazy, I will just let it build up inside. I don't think women are mind readers (if you are, that's really cool). Having pent-up anger and resentment is not good for your relationship, your mate and especially for yourself. It's amazing how much lighter you feel when you get something off your chest. Since I didn't start practicing this until later, I am revoking one medal. When you start hurting yourself, you definitely are not a winner.

So, where were we, at the decline of The Big One? Cable was his best friend, and unless I was wearing a shirt made of fishing lures, he didn't see me. Nothing in common, no marriage in the works, I couldn't even picture what our kids would look like, and I had lots of pent-up anger because of it all. Well, we were seriously starting to drift apart. I guess if I had made a reality TV show about it, he would realize what was happening.

Having nothing else to do at home with The Big One, I resorted to baking! I needed an outlet, something I could just get lost in. I loved whipping up a batch of biscotti. I baked to fill the emotional void this relationship was creating. For that I get a baking ribbon, just because.

I would have endless conversations with friends asking for advice. I wasn't sure what to do. It was my best friend Nikki Rae who said, "I don't know what to say to make it better, Erin, but we have been having this conversation for two years now." Two years! OMG, she was right. We needed to fix this relationship or end it. It couldn't keep going on this way. A colleague once asked me, "Would you be friends with The Big One if he weren't your boyfriend?" That question really stuck in my mind. I wouldn't be friends with him because we had nothing in common anymore. I'd done a lot of growing up in my twenties. Instead of growing together, we'd grown apart.

Was this it? Was this how all long-term relationships ended up? No fizzle, no spark, no conversation, no nuthin'? Just lots of biscotti and profiterole rolls? Well, it was time to shut'er down then. Maybe this would have been a good relationship for a mime, but I was far from a mime.

But, even after the countless conversations with friends I did not shut it down. I stayed with The Big One. I guess I was too scared, too comfortable, too nervous about being on my own. I had been in this relationship for more than six years now. I think I'd forgotten how to be independent. I'd lost my balls. How could a feisty redhead with an Aries moon sign forget how to be independent? I know. It was probably because Cancer is my sun sign. Cancers love the home environment; we get comfortable easily. We love caring for people and change a lot of ourselves to adapt to whatever environment we are in. Well, this adapting served him plenty but not me.

You know, when I thought about it, it didn't even serve him well because there was a much better match for him out there. I really cared for The Big One. I wanted him to be happy. He may not have known it right then, but he would have been much better off with someone else. I don't think it takes two halves to make a whole. It takes two wholes to have a successful relationship. I needed to find my own personal other half and get my balls back.

The final breakup process started happening without me even knowing it. I had this overwhelming feeling of jazzing up my appearance. I started growing my hair (The Big One liked it short). I started getting in shape and shedding my happy twenty pounds. I no longer resented all our friends getting married and having babies before us (even though we had been dating longer). I just wanted to be me again.

In the final year of our relationship, we had a serious talk about what we needed to do to make it work. I don't think a threesome with Brad Pitt could have saved it.

We went on our last vacation in May. It was the "holy sh-t balls, I can't believe we are still together, we are so over, if we weren't driving beside a cliff I would jump out of this moving vehicle" vacation. The way he moved, breathed, ate drove me crazy and vice versa. The relationship wasn't even comfortable anymore. Why were we staying together? Was there some mysterious prize I didn't know about for the one who held out the longest?

On that vacation, I had quietly decided in my mind that the relationship was over. This quiet decision stayed in my mind all summer. Man, the words *It's over* are not easy to say, at all. Why couldn't The Big One have said it first? He had to be thinking it, too. I would have totally understood if he did. I would have just given him a high five, said "Thanks for the last seven years" and have been on my merry way. After all, he wasn't a bad guy, just the wrong one. Maybe I could've said, "I'm an alien and I have to return to 'Planet Leave You' immediately." No, that wouldn't work. I needed to be strong and just be honest with him.

I'd talked to some experienced people who'd told me there was usually one "A-ha" moment that just made you realize there was no turning back. My moment was when my beloved Gramps passed away. He was a country rock star with more personality than Minnie Pearl. I'd returned home for his funeral, alone. Everyone was asking, "Where's The Big One?" Hmm…I hadn't even thought to ask him to come. But should I need to ask him? Shouldn't he have known just to come with me? When I returned to Toronto, I told him we were living together but we were living completely separate lives. We were basically just roommates. I told The Big One he was no longer "The One" for me. He hadn't seen it coming. Really? You thought our relationship was okay? I had a better relationship with my plants.

About a week later, I packed up my car with as many of my personal belongings as it would hold, including my medals, ribbon and a trophy that read "You guys gave it your best shot, but now it's time to go find your balls." So, off I went, ball-less, terrified, but proud that I didn't end up like so many people before me. It was time to find out what made me happy and what other dating adventures and medals were in store for me.

I must go back to my planet now!!..

HELL-BENT AND BISCOTTI BOUND

MAYBE NOT HELL-BENT BUT I AM READY FOR A LITTLE RECKLESS FUN.

2 ½	cups all-purpose flour
½	cup cocoa
3	tsps. baking powder
½	cup sugar
½	cup brown sugar, packed
¼	cup butter, softened
3	eggs
½	cup semisweet chocolate chips
½	cup white chocolate chips

DRIZZLE

½	cup white chocolate chips
1	tsp. vegetable oil

✪ Preheat oven to 350°F (175°C).

✪ In a medium bowl, sift together flour, cocoa and baking powder.

✪ In a large bowl, combine sugars and butter; beat until well blended.

✪ Add eggs; beat well.

✪ Add flour mixture; stir well. Stir in the white and semisweet chips.

✪ Divide dough in half. On a lined cookie sheet flatten dough to make two rectangles about ½ inch thick. Place a couple inches apart from each other.

✪ Bake for about 25 minutes or until set. Let cool enough to touch. Cut into ½-inch slices. Lay slices on their sides. Continue baking for 5–7 minutes. Turn slices over and bake for an additional 5–7 minutes.

✪ Let cool on wire racks. To dress up your biscotti, melt white chocolate and oil in a small saucepan over low heat. Drizzle over biscotti.

✪ Tip: I like to store my biscotti in a freezer bag in the freezer.

NEWLY SINGLE

After I became single for the first time in seven years, I was drained of every emotion a person has. Considering my sun sign is Cancer, we go through most of these emotions every hour, even on a good day. I would feel alone, excited, giddy and timid, just to name a few. I was pumped about the possible opportunities my future had in store for me. But, I was also nervous because I really didn't know who I was anymore. All I knew was I was The Big One's ex. I knew what I didn't want, and it was time to find out what I did.

After shedding twenty pounds of my own weight and two hundred of the other kind, it was time to feel like me again. I knew I wasn't the same person I was back in my early twenties and I didn't need to be. Each day I felt better and better. I was more alive, more confident, I was slowly getting my balls back, and I couldn't have been happier. Parting ways with The Big One was one of the most difficult decisions I'd ever made, but in the end I knew it was the right one for both of us.

Sure, our relationship ended a few years later than it should have, but I needed to do it in my own time. I learned that sometimes people are meant to be in your life for a short time. This relationship was a great accomplishment for me. I got over my phobia of commitment. Well, pretty close to it.

I moved into my new bachelor pad. It was small, but it was all mine. I could listen to country music as loud as I wanted. Do my dishes when I wanted to. Hang whatever picture up that I wanted. For the first time in almost seven years, it was all about me. I didn't really feel I was being selfish, I was just figuring out what made me *me*.

I never felt more alone, though, than I did the first time I slept in my new apartment. Although I had not lived at home since I was eighteen, I'd always had a roommate. It was scary being all by myself. Just me and my Erin Beanie Baby, sleeping on an air mattress, watching the gleam of the full moon bounce off my trophy and wondering if this was going to get easier. Had I really made the right decision?

It did get much easier, and I really started to feel like a real person again. I stopped feeling numb and began going through the motions of everyday life. Many of us tend to adapt to our partners' needs instead of our own, at the expense of our personal happiness. I'd just wanted to make him happy, so if he didn't like something I was doing (i.e. partying with my girlfriends, wearing my style of clothes, peeing behind bushes), I changed. It was time to change back. I was ready to pee wherever I wanted. My hair was longer than it had been in years. I stopped dressing conservatively and started getting my mojo back.

It was great to hear my friends say, "Erin is back!" I felt so rejuvenated. Over the months, my calendar was full of concerts and parties and brunches. It felt good to flirt, dress sexy and hang out with all my buddies. I had a lot of years to make up for. I even kissed three guys in one night, pretty impressive for me. This girl was ready for some serious flirting.

I had a blast making up for lost time. Occasionally, I would have a moment of weakness, though. There were many times I wished I had a partner. For instance, I don't even think twice about going to the movies on my own now, but I can still remember one of the first times I did. It took a lot of courage to do it. Here I am at the theater, with way too much popcorn and cola (why are they so big?). I realized after I'd purchased it that it was not for a newly single gal. I even put two straws in my drink so that people would think that I was sharing with someone else. I sat down kind of feeling like a knob. Then, one couple asks if the seat to my right is taken."Nope," I say. Then another one asks if the seat to my left is taken…awesome, now people really know I'm on my own. I'm like, "No it's not taken, I'm single. I've got no one. And, yes, I'm eating a large popcorn all by myself. You got a problem with it?"

After I gained a little confidence and realized lots of people go to the movies on their own, I now really enjoy it. I rarely go with someone else. I get to watch whatever movie I want, sit wherever I want to sit, stuff my face with popcorn. Admit one newly single gal, please, preferably beside a hot single guy.

NEWLY SINGLE, TOFFEE CHOCOLATE POPCORN

THIS RECIPE IS SO GOOD. YOU WILL BE HAPPY YOU ARE SINGLE, JUST SO YOU DON'T HAVE TO SHARE IT.

1	cup semisweet chocolate chips
½	cup dark corn syrup
¼	cup butter
8	cups popped popcorn (about ½ cup popping kernels)
⅓	cup toffee baking bits

- ✪ Preheat oven to 300°F (150°C).

- ✪ Place popped popcorn in an 9 x 13-inch rectangle baking dish.

- ✪ In a medium saucepan over medium-high heat, bring chocolate chips, corn syrup and butter to a boil; stirring often.

- ✪ Pour over popcorn and stir until evenly coated.

- ✪ Stir in toffee baking bits.

- ✪ Bake in preheated oven for 45 minutes, stirring every 15 minutes.

- ✪ Let cool.

NO MAN REQUIRED

SHORT ON LOVE, NOT ON SHORTBREAD

Here's a straightforward, uncomplicated recipe, to make up for the last guy.

½   **cup cornstarch**

½   **cup confectioners' sugar**

1¼   **cups all-purpose flour**

1   **cup butter, softened**

pinch of salt

- Preheat oven to 275°F (135°C).

- In a medium bowl, sift together cornstarch, confectioners' sugar, salt and flour. Add butter; stir until smooth dough is formed.

- Line a cookie sheet with parchment paper. Roll dough into 1-inch balls. Place 2 inches apart on cookie sheet. Flatten with your fingers or a fork. Decorate with seasonal sprinkles.

- Bake for 20–22 minutes until edges are lightly brown.

- Tip: I like to put ⅓ cup of mini semisweet chocolate chips in half of the dough, to mix it up a little.

ERIN'S GO-TO COOKIE

SOMETIMES YOU DON'T KNOW WHY YOU'RE EMOTIONAL. YOU JUST ARE. BUT WHAT YOU DO KNOW IS YOU MUST BAKE SOMETHING NOW! THIS IS MY GO-TO recipe. IT'S GOT a LITTLE BIT OF EVERYTHING.

½	cup sugar
½	cup brown sugar, packed
½	cup butter, softened
½	cup smooth peanut butter
1	tsp. vanilla extract
1	egg
¾	cup all-purpose flour
¾	cup quick-cooking oats
1	tsp. baking soda
½	tsp. salt
1	cup semisweet chocolate chips
½	cup coconut

✪ Preheat oven to 375°F (190°C).

✪ In a large bowl, combine sugars and butter; beat until light and fluffy. Add peanut butter, vanilla and egg; mix well. Stir in flour, oats, baking soda and salt. Stir in chocolate chips and coconut.

✪ Drop by tablespoonfuls onto a lined cookie sheet, 2 inches apart. Flatten with fingers.

✪ Bake for 10–12 minutes until golden brown. Let cool on wire racks.

WHY IS MOM ALWAYS RIGHT?

You know that one guy your mother instantly dislikes? The one you fall head over heels for even though she greatly disapproves? Well, she's recently divorced, so she wouldn't like any man right now—not even George Clooney! But she insists it's not because of her recent breakup and you should stop dating this man immediately. Well, of course I have to prove my mother wrong. That's what we daughters do. This guy isn't the bad apple she is making him out to be. Okay, maybe he's a little sour, but who doesn't like a bit of a bad boy?

Maybe my mom was right when she said not to tease my bangs for every high school photo. Maybe my mom was right when she warned me that my teenage bad-boy rocker boyfriend would smash my heart into a million pieces. She can't be right about everything…can she?

He was the first man I'd met in the city who owned power tools and knew how to use them. He had a Paul Bunyan build, but instead of an axe and an ox, he had a hammer drill and a pick-up truck. This was comforting to me because growing up in the country you are basically born with power tools in your hand. Not to mention that every man has at least one vehicle.

So what if my guy didn't call when he said he would…he was faithful, right? So what if he canceled plans all the time…he was just busy with work, right? I'm an understanding kind of girlfriend. I know how sometimes life can get in the way of life. He said everything I wanted to hear, and I'd eat it up. Oh, it was so nice to finally meet a man who knew my needs and understood me.

After a couple of months, my instincts started telling me, that boy ain't right. I just had this uneasy feeling in my stomach, constantly. I'm very intuitive, and my intuition was questioning all his motives. I had a feeling his "power tools" were spread around the city. I don't think I was the only woman who benefited from his handy ways. I stopped trusting him. And, when you don't have trust in a relationship, it's really time to throw in the towel. One day my best friend Nikki Rae called and asked me what I was doing. "Oh, just scouring the streets of Toronto looking for his vehicle," I said. He hadn't come over when he'd said he would—again. So, I was determined to find him and ask him why. She quickly brought to my attention that I was acting "loco" and that I should reevaluate my situation with him.

Well, easier said than done. He was the kind of guy who got under your skin. All of my thoughts were consumed by him. After months of hearing the talk, I figured it was just a matter of time before he made good on his promises of happily ever after. He'd promised me the world, and I was just waiting for him to show it to me. It was like I needed to win his affection or I just couldn't get on with my life. I stopped going to the gym. What if he called while I was out? I completely zoned out of conversations I had with my friends because my mind was always on him. "I must stay home and put every ounce of energy I have into him. I must sit by the phone and wait for his call. So what if my svelte tummy is getting a little flabby? It's not like anybody's going to see it. I never go out anymore," I told myself.

After a few months of broken dates, minimal phone calls and going loco, I decided the relationship was not living up to my expectations and that I deserved better. He said he cared about me so much. If he did, then why did he make me feel so awful all the time? The man was not going to let me go. He is the type that requires the attention of lots of ladies because he is so insecure. He promises you the world so you get hooked on him, but never delivers.

I finally said enough is enough. Actions speak louder than words, and his actions were saying nuthin' but dump his sorry ass. So, I did. I had to do it cold turkey. I had to cut off all contact with the man because even the slightest contact was grounds for a relapse. I felt really strong after, and I'd learned yet another valuable lesson from relationships: Do not date people that make you LOCO! And yes, Mother, you were (usually, always) right again! You can stop smiling now. Well, at least I haven't teased my bangs since 1991.

ERIN BOLGER

MY MOM IS ALWAYS RIGHT
CHOCA-MOCHA SQUARES

THIS IS a recipe my mother passed on to me, among other things.

2	tbsps. cocoa
½	cup sugar
1	egg
½	cup butter
1	tsp. vanilla
2	cups graham cracker crumbs
½	cup almond slivers, roasted at 325°F (160°C) for 5–7 minutes.

- These are no-bake squares.

- Combine cocoa, sugar and egg in a medium saucepan; mix well.

- Add butter; stir frequently over medium heat until bubbly.

- Remove from heat, add vanilla and nuts; mix well. Gradually add graham cracker crumbs.

- Press into a greased 8-inch-square pan. Let cool.

CHOCA-MOCHA ICING

1	tbsp. butter, softened
1	tbsp. cocoa
1	tbsp. strong hot coffee (or 1 tbsp. hot water/ 1 tsp. instant coffee)
1	cup confectioners' sugar

- Combine the first three ingredients until smooth, then gradually add confectioners' sugar until you get a creamy texture. Spread over cooled squares and refrigerate.

ME AND MY COOKIES ARE SO OVER YOU

Bake these to forget "what's-his-name." The best part of this recipe is smashing the nuts with a hammer. Some people use a rolling pin, I use a hammer. It's the handy girl in me.

- Preheat oven to 375°F (190°C).

- In a large bowl, combine sugars and butter; beat until light and fluffy.

- Add vanilla and eggs; blend well.

- Mix in flour, baking powder, baking soda and salt; stir in chocolate chips, almonds and toffee baking bits.

- Drop by tablespoonfuls onto a lined cookie sheet; bake for about 10 minutes until golden brown. Cool on wire racks.

¾ cup sugar
½ cup brown sugar, packed
¾ cup butter, softened

1 tsp. vanilla extract
2 eggs

2½ cups all-purpose flour
1 tsp. baking powder
½ tsp. baking soda
½ tsp. salt

1 cup semisweet chocolate chips
½ cup toffee baking bits

1 cup almonds. Put almonds in a plastic freezer bag, gently smash with a hammer. I prefer the almonds to be a bit chunky. Roast at 325°F (160°C) for 5–7 minutes.

MY MOM THINKS I'M COOL.
YOU NOT SO MUCH,
BUTTERSCOTCH WAFFLE COOKIES

2   **cups butterscotch chips**
½   **cup semisweet chocolate chips**
1   **cup peanuts**
6   **waffle cones, crushed**

✪ In a medium saucepan over low heat, melt the butterscotch and chocolate chips.

✪ Remove from heat; stir in the peanuts and the crushed waffle cones.

✪ Drop by tablespoonfuls onto a cookie sheet. Refrigerate until set.

BITE MY PEANUT BRITTLE, BI-ATCH

SORRY, I'VE BEEN DRINKING.

1   **cup sugar**

½   **cup dark or light corn syrup (dark will add a more distinctive flavor)**

¼   **tsp. salt**

¼   **cup water**

1   **cup peanuts (raw Spanish peanuts are best)**

2   **tbsps. butter, softened**

1   **tsp. baking soda**

✪ In a large saucepan over medium-high heat, bring sugar, corn syrup, salt and water to a boil.

✪ Stir in peanuts. Clip a candy thermometer to the side of the saucepan. Make sure the thermometer does not touch the bottom of the saucepan. Stir the mixture frequently until the temperature reaches 300°F (150°C).

✪ Remove from heat; right away add the butter and baking soda. Mixture will foam up. Pour onto a lined cookie sheet; spread mixture to cover cookie sheet. Let cool; break into pieces.

MY MOM
DIDN'T LIKE YOU ANYWAY, CUPCAKE

WELL, SHE DIDN'T...GET OVER IT.

2	cups sugar
¾	cup cocoa powder
2	cups all-purpose flour
1	tsp. baking powder
2	tsps. baking soda
1	tsp. salt
2	eggs
¾	cup vegetable oil
2	tsps. vanilla extract
1	cup buttermilk
1	cup boiling water

- Preheat oven to 350°F (175°C).

- Line cupcake tin, makes 18 cupcakes.

- In a large bowl, sift together dry ingredients. Add eggs, vegetable oil, vanilla and buttermilk. Beat with a mixer on medium speed for a couple of minutes until smooth and silky. Stir in boiling water until blended.

- Fill muffin tins with batter; bake in oven for 22–25 minutes.

MOM'S BEST EVER ICING

¼	cup butter, softened
2	tbsps. cocoa powder
2	tbsps. hot water
2	cups confectioners' sugar

- Combine the butter, cocoa and hot water. Gradually add the confectioners' sugar until smooth and creamy. Ice cupcakes and enjoy!

I'M SO DONE WITH YOU AND THE HORSE YOU RODE IN ON, HAYSTACK COOKIES

Here's my take on an oldie but a goodie.

| 1 | cup butterscotch chips |
| 2 | cups semisweet chocolate chips |

| 3 | cups salted pretzel sticks, broken into small pieces, excess salt removed |
| 2 | cups mini marshmallows |

✿ In a medium saucepan over low heat, melt the butterscotch and chocolate chips.

✿ Remove from heat; stir in broken pretzels, and marshmallows.

✿ Drop by tablespoonfuls onto a lined cookie sheet. Refrigerate until set.

THE BIG HURT

You know the Big Hurt, the one where you shout, "I WILL NEVER LOVE AGAIN." Where you lock yourself up in your place watching every girly, sappy movie you can find, only to emerge to buy more wine and baking ingredients. Yep, that's the one. I've been there, too, more than once. You never get used to the feeling, like you've been punched in the stomach and you can't catch your breath.

It's always just when you think everything is going great with your guy and then, out of the blue, he drops a doozy and says it's over. You replay the last few days over and over in your head, wondering why you didn't see it coming. The truth is there was probably nothing to analyze. He charms you, gets close to you and then when he feels he is getting too close, he runs away from fear of commitment. My friend has a name for these guys, which I think is inappropriate to mention here (you know my family is going to read this).

Afterward, you feel like you can never trust anyone again or ever let your guard down. I mean, that's what we do when we get hurt, right? But, like every amazing woman out there, we take a few days to regroup, and reenter the world realizing he was just a giant _____ (fill in the blank), and you're lucky you're not with the giant _____ anymore. Your heart may still be shattered, but you are on the mend. The hundred-pound weight on your chest gets lighter with every day. Yes, I've lost sleep, almost quit my job and cried on the floor of a public bathroom (it was relatively clean).

I can definitely say I am a much stronger person now. After each dating experience I get more comfortable with who I am as a person. You might think it was a big waste of time dating what's-his-face, but every life adventure makes you the person you are, and I'm pretty happy with myself. I don't regret any of it. I'm even willing to keep dating!

So, pick yourself up off that bathroom floor, bake some cookies and be happy that you are not with a man that doesn't know how awesome you truly are. And to all you giant _____ out there, thank you for making this chapter possible. And, oh yeah, no cheesecake for you!!!!

WANTED

The Cookie Gang

REWARD

Broken Heart Mending

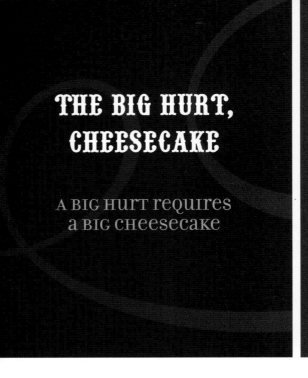

THE BIG HURT, CHEESECAKE

A BIG HURT requires
a BIG cheesecake

1	cup finely crushed ginger cookies
¼	cup butter, melted
3	8 oz. packages cream cheese, softened
1	cup sugar
1	tbsp. all-purpose flour
1	tsp. ground ginger
1	tsp. lemon juice
1	tsp. vanilla extract
½	tsp. salt
3	eggs, slightly beaten
⅓	cup caramel sauce

- ✪ Preheat oven to 350°F (175°C).

- ✪ Cut a piece of parchment paper to fit the bottom of a 9-inch springform pan.

- ✪ Mix crushed cookies and melted butter together. Press into prepared pan. Bake for 5 minutes.

- ✪ In a large bowl, beat cream cheese with a mixer until smooth. Beat in sugar, flour, ginger, lemon juice, vanilla and salt.

- ✪ Stir in eggs. Beat until smooth. Pour mixture on top of crust.

- ✪ Bake 45 minutes or until center is set. Let cool completely on a wire rack. Refrigerate.

- ✪ Just before you are ready to serve, spoon caramel topping over the cheesecake.

I'M PRETTY AWESOME, YUM YUM SQUARES

I come from a long line of awesome ladies. This recipe was passed down from one of them.

½	cup butter, softened
2	tbsps. brown sugar
1¼	cups all-purpose flour
2	eggs, well beaten
½	tsp. salt
1	tsp. vanilla
1	cup brown sugar, packed
1	cup coconut
1	cup walnut pieces

- ✪ Preheat oven at 350°F (175°C).

- ✪ Mix butter and 2 tbsp. brown sugar until light and fluffy, stir in flour. Press into an 8-inch square pan.

- ✪ Combine eggs, salt, vanilla and remaining brown sugar; mix well. Stir in coconut and walnuts, spread on top of crust.

- ✪ Bake for 20 minutes or until top is golden brown.

YOU CAN KISS MY
TRIPLE DECKER CARROT CAKE
GOODBYE

IT ISN'T YOURS FOR THE TAKING anymore.

2	cups all-purpose flour
2	tsps. baking powder
1 ½	tsps. baking soda
1	tsp. salt
2	tsps. cinnamon
2	cups sugar
1½	cups vegetable oil
4	eggs
2	cups finely grated carrots
1	cup crushed pineapple, drained
1	cup walnuts, chopped
1	cup coconut

- Preheat oven to 350°F (175°C). Grease and flour three 9-inch-round cake pans.

- In a large mixing bowl, sift together flour, baking powder, baking soda, salt and cinnamon.

- Add sugar, oil and eggs; mix together for 3 minutes with a hand mixer.

- Stir in carrots, pineapple, chopped nuts and coconut.

- Pour into prepared pans. Bake in preheated oven for 35 minutes or until center is set.

CREAM CHEESE ICING

½	cup butter, softened
1	8 oz. package cream cheese, softened
1	tsp. vanilla extract
5	cups confectioners' sugar
¼	cup toasted coconut for decorating. Bake at 300°F (150°C) for about 5 minutes or until coconut is a light golden brown; stir often.

- Cream together butter and cream cheese. Add the vanilla. Stir in the confectioners' sugar.

- Spread evenly on the top of the first layer. Add the second layer, spread evenly on that layer. Add third layer; spread icing evenly all over cake. Sprinkle with toasted coconut.

- Refrigerate.

I NEED A REAL MAN, MAPLE PUMPKIN PIE

I USED TO THINK PUMPKIN PIE WAS NOT SOMETHING YOU ATE TO GET OVER A MAN. BOY, WAS I WRONG. IT'S NOW ONE OF MY FAVORITES.

1	small sugar pumpkin
If you really must, use 1½ cups of canned pumpkin. But please don't tell me.
¼	cup butter
¼	cup brown sugar
1¼	cups graham cracker crumbs
¾	cup brown sugar
1¼	tsps. cinnamon
1	tsp. ginger
1	tsp. nutmeg
¼	tsp. ground cloves
½	tsp. salt
⅔	cup real maple syrup (medium grade)
1¼	cups light half-and-half
3	eggs

✪ Preheat oven to 375°F (190°C).

✪ Split pumpkin, remove seeds and scrape out inside of the pumpkin. Place the two pumpkin halves in a large baking pan facedown; cover with foil. Bake for 1 hour or until quite soft. Remove from the oven and let cool. Change the oven temperature to 350°F (175°C).

✪ Melt butter in a medium saucepan; add brown sugar; mix well. Add graham cracker crumbs. Press into 9-inch pie plate.

✪ Remove pumpkin skin and discard. Puree pumpkin in a blender or use a hand blender.

✪ Measure 1½ cups of pumpkin, place in a mixing bowl. Add brown sugar, cinnamon, nutmeg, ginger, cloves and salt. Stir in maple syrup and half-and-half. Stir in eggs one at a time. Pour filling on top of crust.

✪ Bake for 1 hour or until center is set.

BEST FRIENDS FOREVER, OATMEAL CHOCOLATE CHIP COOKIES

IF ALL ELSE FAILS, I STILL HAVE YOU.

¾	cup brown sugar, packed
½	cup sugar
1	cup butter, softened
2	eggs
1	tsp. vanilla extract
1½	cups all-purpose flour
½	tsp. salt
1	tsp. baking powder
½	tsp. baking soda
1	cup quick cooking oats
1	cup semisweet chocolate chips

- ✪ Preheat oven to 375°F (175°C).

- ✪ Blend together sugars and butter until light and fluffy. Add eggs and vanilla; mix well.

- ✪ In a separate bowl, sift together flour, salt, baking powder and baking soda. Add to wet mixture; combine together.

- ✪ Stir in oats and chocolate chips. Drop by tablespoonfuls onto a lined cookie sheet. Bake for 8–10 minutes, until golden brown.

You know the best thing I love about desserts, other than that they taste amazing? They are the perfect companions. They give constant love and support, no matter what life throws at you. They never lie, cheat, complain or snore. They always smell great. They show up on time. They never make you cry unless they're tears of joy because they taste so good. The only downfall is they can add some junk to your trunk, but that's what fitness trainers are for, right?

Anyway, I would just like to thank all the desserts in my life that have helped me through some of life's not-so-sweet situations. I couldn't have done it without you, especially you, oatmeal chocolate chip cookie. You have been with me since the very beginning.

CHAPTER 3

The Good, The Bad & The Fugly

A POTLUCK OF DATING SHENANIGANS

I'M NOT DUTCH, APPLE CRISP

YES, I'M AN INDEPENDENT SUCCESSFUL WOMAN BUT DON'T WORRY, I WON'T BE OFFENDED IF YOU PAY FOR DINNER!

4	cups apples, peeled, cored and sliced in small pieces (I prefer McIntosh apples)
1	tbsp. lemon juice
1½	cups frozen cranberries, thawed
½	cup sugar
1	tsp. cinnamon

TOPPING

⅓	cup all-purpose flour
⅓	cup butter, softened
½	cup brown sugar
1	cup rolled oats
½	tsp. salt

✪ Preheat oven to 375°F (190°C). Grease an 8- or 9-inch-square baking dish.

✪ In a large bowl, combine apples, lemon juice, cranberries, sugar and cinnamon. Pour into prepared dish.

✪ In a medium bowl, cream together the flour, butter and brown sugar; mix well. Stir in the oats and salt. Sprinkle evenly over fruit mixture.

✪ Bake for 40 minutes or until fruit is tender and topping is browned.

SURFING FOR LOVE

After my long-term relationship ended and I'd gotten all of that reckless fun out of my system, it was time for some real adult dating. By real, I mean online dating. Yep, I decided to try it out like so many friends and colleagues had before me. It was a little overwhelming at first. Making a profile is much harder than it seems. I didn't know how to describe myself in a short paragraph and come up with a headline that would grab someone's attention. I needed something more than "I'm pretty awesome and I'm a baker." After I finally finished a catchy little paragraph and had a poser photo shoot down by the beach, I was ready to launch my online dating career.

After only one day I had forty responses! At first, I couldn't handle all the attention. I felt bad if I didn't reply to people, even if I wasn't interested. There should be an automatic "thanks for checking me out, but you are just not my type" message. Then, there was the instant messaging system I had to get used to. I have a hard enough time typing, let alone chatting with three guys at once. I had to learn the entire Internet lingo. This was new to me. I thought "LOL" meant "Lots of Love" and that all those guys I barely knew were sending me weird messages…ha ha…"LMFAO."

After a few days of chatting, it was time to get out of the virtual world and meet the guys. I probably went on twenty dates that summer. I was beginning to regret writing "I like beers on a patio" in my profile. My stomach was morphing into a small beer gut. I met up with guys from all walks of life. The Artist, the Banker, the Lawyer, the Cowboy, the Athlete, the Computer Geek and the Musician…nothing really panned out for me, though. I think that three was the most number of dates I had with one single guy. Not sure why; it was like my potentials and I were always looking for something else, I guess because there were so many options. Sometimes it would be frustrating, though, especially when I met someone and I thought there was a connection. The date would go well, and I would think, "Okay, I like this guy; maybe he will call me for a second date." So I'd go home and, of course, check out his pictures on his profile and he'd be online too. Since he didn't instant message me to say, "Hey," I knew he was surfing for someone else without even giving me a chance! Well, another girl's just a mouse click away. So why not, when we are that easily accessible? I guess with so many fish in the sea he wondered what else he could catch and threw me back in the ocean.

So, after many first dates, my online dating career ended after the summer. I wasn't fired, I just gave my notice. I deleted my account and never looked back. I've heard countless stories of people hooking up and even getting married from such services. To be honest, I think I believe too much in destiny. Online dating seems forced to me. Dates ended up feeling more like an interview than an actual date. I feel like my first encounter with my Knight in Shining Armor should be accidental. Like: he trips on the street and accidentally throws his mocha latte all over me and it's love at first coffee… something like that. But until that day comes, I'm up for trying new ways of meeting people. Okay, occasionally when I've had too much wine and I am feeling a little lonely I make up a profile, only to delete it a little later when the effects of my vino have worn off.

It wasn't a total loss though. My Internet lingo has improved greatly. I feel really confident going on first dates now. I don't take five hours primping and priming for them like I did before the computer entered my life and don't build them up in my mind as much. It's just two people meeting to see what possibilities they may have. Don't let my experience discourage you. Good luck surfing, I hope you catch a good wave, "TTYL."

WANTED

THE BISCOTTI BANDITS

** REWARD **

ABSOLUTELY

INTERNET DATING FONDUE

A great way to try many different chocolate combinations.

2   **cups 50% dark chocolate chips or 1 12 oz. 50% dark chocolate bar**

½   **cup whipping cream**

1   **tbsp. strong instant coffee**

½   **tsp. vanilla**

½   **tsp. cinnamon. I love a little cinnamon in my chocolate.**

✪ In a medium saucepan, over low heat, melt chocolate, cream, coffee, vanilla and cinnamon; mix well.

✪ Transfer the mixture to a fondue pot. Try to experiment with what you dip. Of course fruit is amazing, but so are marshmallows, pretzels, red licorice and the occasional man.

I FORGOT TO MENTION I WAS MARRIED, BLUEBERRY CHEESECAKE

HOW can THAT SLIP a man's mind?

½ cup butter

⅓ cup brown sugar

2½ cups graham cracker crumbs

1 8 oz. package cream cheese, softened

½ cup confectioners' sugar

2 cups whipped topping, frozen

1 can blueberry pie filling

✪ Melt butter and sugar in a saucepan over low heat. Stir in graham cracker crumbs, setting aside ¼ cup of mixture.

✪ Press into a 9 x 12-inch pan. Let crust cool in fridge.

✪ Blend cream cheese and confectioners' sugar together until smooth. Stir in frozen whipped topping; blend well.

✪ Spread over cooled crust. Let set in fridge for 30 minutes.

✪ Spread pie filling on top and sprinkle with remaining graham cracker crumb mixture. Refrigerate.

SPEED-DATING CHALLENGE

What could be more exciting than chatting with some twenty-odd guys, all in one evening? Hmm, I don't know, watching my mother read a book (she reads a lot). Originally, speed dating did sound like a fun way to meet an array of men. My friend Jo and I signed up for the event. It was held at a restaurant with a bunch of tables set up, some snacks and, of course, a bell and a stopwatch.

I never know when to arrive for singles gatherings such as this. Do you show up early but risk the fact that you may look a little eager? Though my reason would be to get good snacks before they are all picked over. Or, do you arrive fashionably late and miss out on good snacks and good seating? Jo and I had to make sure we got seats side by side so we could "tee hee" about how silly we felt.

We arrived somewhere in the middle, which was still too early as there were not many people there. Oh well, at least we were able to scope out all the possible suitors as they walked through the door. Maybe we would each meet our Mr. Awesome tonight.

After I enjoyed a helping of cheesy nachos, it came time to get myself situated at a table and hear the rules of the evening:

1} Find yourself a seat.

2} You have three-minute conversations with every guy.

3} When you hear the sound of the bell, the guy moves to the next table to his right.

4} Jot down your picks of the night and hope for a match.

Okay, This was pretty straightforward. I'm good at talking, so I wasn't feeling too intimidated. It was up to the guys to sit down at their first table. The best way I can describe the way I felt was as a kid, when you were waiting to be picked for the baseball team, hoping not to be the last one. We all know what that means. It did take a while for someone to sit down. Either I'm really ugly or guys are intimidated by me. Maybe they were saving the best for last. Yeah, that was it! So, after what seemed like forever, someone sat across from me. Then the bell rang and our three-minute conversation began. Then, another ding. Even if you were only halfway through a story, the guys had to move to the next table. Sometimes that ding was a saving grace. In most cases, it was. I had the same conversation with pretty much all the guys: "What do you do for a living? Did you grow up in Toronto? Do you have any pets?" Boring. Not to mention, none of the guys tickled my fancy. Obviously with such little conversation going on, this type of dating was based more on looks and attraction. I felt like such an idiot when I asked this one slightly nerdy guy where his accent was from. He didn't have one. He just had a unique voice and a unique face after he turned red from me asking that.

Guy after guy, ding after ding, everyone started blurring together. I wondered when this night would end. Had I wasted my hard-earned cash on some cheesy nachos and repetitive conversations? Losing interest, I began scanning the room and realized all the guys were less than average but every woman there was stylish, beautiful and just really put together. I couldn't believe there were so many of us! We should start a union. For a moment, I contemplated dating one of the girls; maybe we would be a perfect match. But since I'm straight I knew that would never work. Oh well, let the search continue…ding.

SPEED-DATING QUICKIES

SPEED DATING - QUICK AND PAINLESS MAYBE.
STILL WORTH BAKING SOMETHING FOR. JUST NOT WORTH
SPENDING A LOT OF TIME DOING IT.

1	cup sugar
1	cup brown sugar
1	cup butter
1	cup milk (1 or 2%)
1	tsp. vanilla extract
2	cups semisweet chocolate chips
4	cups quick-cooking oats
1	cup flaked coconut

○ In a medium saucepan, bring sugars, butter and milk to a boil over medium heat.

○ Remove from heat; add vanilla.

○ Stir in chocolate chips; mix until melted. Add oats and coconut; combine.

○ Drop by tablespoonfuls onto a lined cookie sheet. Refrigerate until set.

QUALITY NOT QUANTITY,
CHOCOLATE DIPPED STRAWBERRIES

MORE ISN'T ALWAYS BETTER. SOMETIMES YOU JUST END UP WITH A CONSTANT DINGING IN YOUR HEAD.

6	oz. white chocolate
8	oz. semisweet chocolate
14	large strawberries, with stems

DRIZZLE

2	oz. white chocolate
½	tsp. vegetable oil.

✪ Melt the white and semisweet chocolate in separate small saucepans over low heat. Have fun and dip the strawberries however you like. Let cool and set in the refrigerator.

✪ Melt the white chocolate and stir in the oil. Drizzle over strawberries.

GOODBYE MEN, HELLO DOLLY SQUARES

OKAY, MAYBE I'M NOT GOING TO SWITCH TEAMS. WHO'S TO SAY IT HASN'T CROSSED MY MIND THOUGH!

½	cup butter, melted
2	cups graham cracker crumbs
1	cup coconut
1	cup semisweet chocolate chips
1	cup chopped walnuts
10	oz. can sweetened condensed milk

- ✪ Preheat oven to 350°F (175°C) degrees.
- ✪ Mix butter and crumbs together. Place in a 9 x 13-inch baking dish; press firmly.
- ✪ Sprinkle coconut, chocolate chips and walnuts evenly over base.
- ✪ Pour condensed milk over top of the above ingredients.
- ✪ Bake for 25 minutes. Cool and cut into squares.

MAYBE IT'S DESTINY,
DREAM BARS

THE WRITING'S IN THE STARS AND IN THIS CHOCOLATY PEANUT BUTTER BAR.

2	cups sugar
1	cup butter, softened
1½	tsp. vanilla extract
4	eggs, slightly beaten
1¼	cups all-purpose flour
¾	cup cocoa powder

TOPPING

10	oz. can sweetened condensed milk
¾	cup semisweet chocolate chips
¾	cup peanut butter chips

- Preheat oven to 350°F (175°C). Grease an 11 x 14-inch baking dish.

- In a large bowl, mix sugar, butter and vanilla until light and fluffy.

- Add eggs; beat until smooth.

- Stir in flour and cocoa to egg mixture; blend well.

- Spread mixture into prepared dish.

- For the topping, combine the condensed milk, chocolate chips and peanut butter chips. Spread evenly over base.

- Bake 30–35 minutes until topping is set and lightly golden. Let cool and enjoy.

GYPSIES, TRAMPS AND GUYS

I'm sure we've all had those moments where we wish we could see ourselves in the future. To know that all the heartache and awful dates you've been through have all been worth it, that we needed to go through all that to appreciate the amazing man we finally found. What's next best to having a crystal ball? A trusted psychic! It took a while to find a psychic who could read me. I've been to a few in the past, and they have been far from right about anything. I've had a reading in a trailer park and even a psychic reading party at my place right before The Big One and I ended. He told me that I was in a great relationship that was destined for a great future. That couldn't have been further from the truth.

Now I go to the same psychic once a year. I found someone who gives me great readings. He was a referral from two people, from two different places of work. So, it has to be fate, right? I still remember our first reading. It was a longer drive than I expected, but it was worth it. I was excited and a little lightheaded, as I pondered what my future had in store for me. He had a British accent, which makes everything sound more official. I wrote down every word he said and underlined the good stuff. We seemed to connect, and I liked what he had to say. So I've continued my readings with him for the past five years. My life is sounding pretty good. Married quicker than I think, two kids, two passports, two homes, two businesses and lots of money. But where is this guy who's going to share this amazing life with me?

The last time I had a reading my psychic said to me, "You haven't met your man yet? You should have!" and "You may have met him already, fleetingly." Great, now I'm wondering, who is this guy? Do I know him? Have we met? I met Joey McIntyre fleetingly this past spring—maybe it's him (if you call following him around town while NKOTB were in town performing *fleetingly*).

Over the years, a lot of what this psychic said has actually come true. I bought a condo, like he predicted, in a high-rise. He even knew the month I would be moving in. Then again I think maybe things come true because they are in the back of my mind. I do go over my notes from time to time. One thing he said a year ago was I would be writing books. He could actually see me publishing a book. That I would have a completely different career other than makeup artistry and it would snowball and take over. Odd, I thought, since at the time, I had only read a handful of books. Why on earth would I be writing one? I gave him a weird look. He said firmly, "I see it happening." And here we are. I guess I will never question him again.

So, maybe people can predict your future, or maybe you make it happen. Power of suggestion is an influential thing. One thing I can predict is I will be going again to have a reading. I love it! Maybe next time it will be with my husband on our yacht in the French Riviera, while sipping champagne.

DARK CHOCOLATE COOKIES

MATCHMAKING. YEP, I'VE TRIED THAT, TOO.
I THINK I'LL STICK TO THESE COOKIES, INSTEAD.

¾	cup butter, softened
¾	cup sugar
½	cup brown sugar, packed
1	tsp. vanilla extract
2	eggs
1¾	cups all-purpose flour
½	cup cocoa powder
1	tsp. baking soda
1	tsp. baking powder
½	tsp. salt
1	cup semisweet chocolate chips
½	cup white chocolate chips

- Preheat oven to 375°F (190°C).

- In a large bowl, mix butter and sugars until light and fluffy.

- Add vanilla and eggs; blend well.

- In a medium bowl, sift together flour, cocoa, baking soda, baking powder and salt. Add to wet mixture. Stirring until just blended.

- Stir in chocolate chips. Roll into 1-inch balls, place 2 inches apart on a lined cookie sheet. Flatten with fingers. Bake for 10–12 minutes.

DATING AIN'T EASY,
GINGERBREAD BISCOTTI

DATING MAY NOT BE EASY, BUT IT SURE IS ENTERTAINING.

⅓	cup vegetable oil
1	cup sugar
3	eggs
¼	cup cooking molasses
3	cups all-purpose flour
1	tbsp. baking powder
1	tbsp. ground ginger
1	tbsp. cinnamon
1½	tsps. ground cloves
¼	tsp. nutmeg
½	cup white chocolate chips.

- Preheat oven to 375°F (190°C).

- In a large bowl, beat together oil, sugar, eggs and molasses.

- In a medium bowl, sift together flour, baking powder, ginger, cinnamon, cloves and nutmeg. Mix into the wet mixture. Dough will be a little sticky and heavy.

- Divide the dough in half on a lined cookie sheet. With lightly floured hands, shape dough into 2 flattened logs about ½ inch thick.

- Bake for about 25 minutes, until center is set. Remove from oven. When cool enough to touch, cut into ½-inch slices. Lay the slices on their sides. Bake for an additional 6–8 minutes. Turn slices over and continue baking for 6–8 minutes.

- In a small saucepan over very low heat, melt the white chocolate chips. Drizzle over baked biscotti.

DATING RULES (FOR THE GUYS)

I have been on my fair share of dates.
So, I thought I would share certain turnoffs I've encountered along the way.
I'm sure most of you will agree with me. Guys take note!

RULE #1 Guys, do not talk about your various surgeries while I'm trying to eat my Caesar salad. Not the kind of conversation to have on a first date. I think I actually had an out-of-body experience on that date, just so I could finish my salad.

RULE #2 Do not show me the engine of your car, no matter how cool you think it is. Unless you are storing a box of chocolates under the hood, I just don't care.

RULE #3 Do not tell me you have to go to the hospital for a simple X-ray right before our date, and never call me again. Wrong, on so many levels.

RULE #4 Do not tell me I would be a lot hotter if I lost a couple of pounds. Quite frankly, my booty is worth more than gold in some countries. The man I end up with will appreciate it.

RULE #5 If you think you may be gay, do not go on a date with me. I will not help you figure it out. I have the worst gaydar ever.

All right, guys, I hope you learn something from this. Ladies, I hope you never have to experience any of it. And, may the force be with you. You will need it!

DATING RULES (FOR THE GIRLS)

It's only fair to include dating rules for the girls.
Because I couldn't think of any, I asked a bunch of my male friends for advice.

Here are their…rules?

RULE #1 All we think about is sex on a first date.

RULE #2 …still thinking about sex.

RULE #3 There is not much you could do wrong to take our mind off sex.

RULE #4 That being said, I guess my only rule would be depending on what outcome you want from your date, wear clean underwear and shave. Sorry ladies, this is all I got.

1¼   cups graham cracker crumbs
¼   cup butter, melted

2   8 oz. packages cream cheese, softened
⅔   cup sugar
1   tsp. cornstarch
2   eggs

1   can pie filling of your choice
      (peach, pineapple, cherry etc.)

✿ Preheat oven to 325°F (165°C); line 12 cupcake
  tins. Or use a mini cheesecake tray.

✿ Mix together graham cracker crumbs and melted
  butter. Divide crumb mixture evenly between the
  prepared cupcake tins. Bake for 5 minutes.

✿ Change oven temperature to 350°F (175°C).

✿ Blend cream cheese, sugar and cornstarch
  together. Stir in eggs. Beat on low speed
  with hand mixer until smooth, about 3 minutes
  (fine lumps are okay.)

✿ Divide mixture into the cupcake tins.
  Fill about ⅔ full. Bake for 20–22 minutes.

✿ Cool 3 hours. Refrigerate until ready to eat.
  Right before serving, remove paper liners
  and spoon a little pie filling on top of each
  cheesecake.

½	tsp. salt
3	egg yolks, beaten
2	cups milk, divided
1	tbsp. butter
1	tsp. vanilla extract
2	bananas, sliced
1	9-inch pie shell, baked

YOU BREAK-A MY HEART, I BAKE-A MY PIE

THE ABOVE TO BE SAID WITH an ITALIAN accent.

- ✪ In a bowl, mix together sugar, cornstarch, salt and beaten egg yolks; blend well. Stir in ½ cup milk.

- ✪ In a large saucepan over medium heat, heat remaining milk until it just comes to a simmer. Remove from heat. Gradually add half of the hot milk to the egg yolk mixture. Return the entire egg yolk mixture back to the saucepan. Bring the mixture to a boil over medium heat, stirring constantly. Continue to heat and stir for 2 more minutes; mixture will thicken.

- ✪ Remove from heat and stir in butter and vanilla. Cover and let cool.

- ✪ Pour half of the cooled filling over cooked pie crust. Layer with sliced bananas. Pour the remainder of filling on top. Cover and keep refrigerated. Garnish with whipped cream when ready to serve.

IT'S NOT ME, IT'S YOU,
SEA-SALTED CARAMELS

½   **cup butter**
½   **cup brown sugar, packed**
2   **tbsps. honey**
½   **cup sweetened condensed milk**

1   **cup 50% dark chocolate chips or**
     1 6 oz. 50% dark chocolate bar

1½   **tsps. sea salt, small coarse pieces**

✪ Grease a 9 x 5-inch loaf pan.

✪ In a heavy-bottom saucepan, combine butter, brown sugar, honey and sweetened condensed milk. Over medium-high heat bring to a boil; stir constantly. Boil for 5 minutes. Remove from heat and beat for a couple of minutes. Pour into prepared pan. Cool.

✪ In a medium saucepan over low heat, melt chocolate chips. Spread over cooled caramel. Sprinkle with sea salt.

✪ Let cool and cut into small pieces.

COMPUTER VS. ME: ROUND 1

Raise your hand if you have been broken up with by e-mail? Wow, nice to know I'm not the only one. You start off with the enjoyment of your morning coffee, followed by visions of throwing your computer out the window—not the greatest way to start your day. Truth is, your computer did nothing wrong. Like the saying goes, "Don't shoot the messenger." All right, I may have injured the messenger a little when I slammed my keyboard down. But, it made me feel a bit better.

I had no idea that this is what we are doing now. I can understand if you only have had a couple of dates, but after a few months you would think that any man would have more respect than that. I hate confrontation as much as the next person, but I just try to treat guys the way I wish they would treat me. I've learned that even if I've had one date with someone and I'm not interested in him but he continues to call, I let him know either on the phone or in person, but never by e-mail. It feels good to nip it in the bud instead of ignoring calls and text messages. Though, I must admit this is new for me. Admittedly, I have been that person who ignores the guy just hoping he would finally get the hint. But never has it crossed my mind to break up with someone over e-mail/text. I guess maybe they think if Britney Spears did it, then so can they. If Britney shaved her head and beat up a car with an umbrella, would you do that, too? Enough said.

So, to all the guys out there, next time you want to break up with your girlfriend by e-mail, just remember: yes, breakups suck and nobody likes to be the bad guy but, trust me, we can handle it. You're not the first breakup we've been through and you probably won't be the last. So grow a pair, be a man and break up with her by phone.

You know, this story may seem a little angrier than my other stories. I tried to lighten it up but, quite frankly, I was really pissed off.

I had been dating this man for about two months. We had dated when I was younger but it was just not the right time for us. So, about nine years later and a few months after The Big One, we tried again. Everything was going smoothly and full-steam ahead. I mean, it wasn't like we had anything to be uncomfortable about. We had done this before but now we could just do it better...or so I thought.

I had just sat down at my computer and had begun reading my e-mails. As per usual, there was the daily e-mail from my new beau. Oh, we were like two peas in a pod. Well, this e-mail was different. It started by saying how happy he was that we reconnected and got to spend this special time together, but, although he cared about me, he had fallen in love with one of his coworkers. That e-mail knocked the wind right out of me. I hadn't seen this coming, considering the day before I was in his company, blissfully unaware of it all.

I had thoughts of bitch slapping my computer. That might seem a little harsh, but then, isn't breaking up with someone over the computer after you have known them for over nine years? I think I deserved more than that. I guess he did not think I deserved more than that and felt comfortable enough to dump me by a machine. Woman to machine might work for the Terminator but not us. I was frustrated and hurt. I couldn't have a face-to-face conversation about breaking up. He didn't give me that option. Funny thing was we had been brought back together because of the computer. I had looked my new beau up on Google, and there he was in plain sight, easy to get a hold of. Little did I know the computer would contribute to the start and the end of this relationship. Sometimes, what happened in the past should just stay there.

I may not have slapped my computer, but with the help of a friend, I aggressively typed a provoking reply. This guy was not getting off easy. He responded with a much nastier e-mail, and our Internet breakup continued. After a few more replies, my fingers and brain were exhausted. I discontinued all contact with the man.

I learned a couple valuable lessons out of this short-lived relationship: Do not search for your exes on Google and it's not nice getting dumped by e-mail. So, if you are past the initial first dates with someone and no longer want to see them, let them know. It doesn't necessarily have to be in person, but at the very least, they need to hear it, not read it.

I have yet to be broken up with by a man this way again. But, if it does happen, I certainly won't be throwing my precious new Mac laptop out the window.

I NEED A MAN THAT HAS BIGGER BALLS THAN MY
BANANA BREAD

WHY ARE THERE SO MANY SINGLE, SUCCESSFUL, INDEPENDENT AND SUPER-HOT WOMEN NOWADAYS? REALLY, I'M ASKING. I DON'T GET IT. WHAT I DO GET IS HOW awesome THIS BANANA BREAD IS. I LOVE IT TOASTED WITH A LITTLE APPLE BUTTER.

¼	cup butter, softened
⅔	cup sugar
2	eggs
1	cup mashed ripe bananas
¼	cup applesauce
1⅔	cups all-purpose flour
1	tsp. baking soda
½	tsp. baking powder
1	tsp. cinnamon
½	tsp. salt

- ✪ Preheat oven to 350°F (175°C).

- ✪ In a large bowl, combine butter and sugar until light and fluffy.

- ✪ Mix in eggs, bananas and applesauce.

- ✪ In a separate bowl, sift the flour, baking soda, baking powder, cinnamon and salt. Add to the banana mixture. Stir until just combined.

- ✪ Pour batter into a greased loaf pan; bake for 60 minutes until center is firm. Let cool before cutting into slices.

BRING IT ON, TOFFEE BISCOTTI

YOU KNOW THAT DATING PHASE WHERE YOU JUST SEEM TO ATTRACT EVERY ODDBALL OUT THERE? YOU JUST KEEP WONDERING WHAT ELSE CAN LIFE THROW YOUR WAY AND END UP SHOUTING, "BRING IT ON."

½	cup sugar
½	brown sugar, packed
¾	cup butter, softened
2	eggs
1½	tsps. vanilla extract
2¼	cups all-purpose flour
½	tsp. salt
1	tsp. baking powder
¼	tsp. baking soda
¾	cup toffee baking bits

- Preheat oven to 350°F (175°C).

- Combine sugars and butter; blend well. Add eggs and vanilla; mix well.

- Stir in flour, salt, baking powder and baking soda until just combined. Stir in toffee bits.

- Form dough into 2 logs. Flatten logs into ½-inch thickness, 3 inches apart.

- Bake for 25 minutes or until set. When cool enough to touch, cut into ½-inch strips. Continue baking for 8–10 minutes. Turn strips over and bake for an additional 8–10 minutes.

- Let cool and enjoy.

DATING HEX

So here I am, in my early thirties. I haven't had a really serious relationship in four years. I'm sure the reason is I repeatedly date the same type of guy. Now, as a single gal again, I've resorted back to my old ways by dating bad boys. I wasn't in the mood to waste my time on a guy that didn't turn my crank. And, after years of loving safely, I welcomed a little danger back into my life with open arms. I figured the reason I have such sizzle with a lot of dangerous types is their wicked ways. I've got a soft spot for them. I definitely wouldn't kick James Bond out of bed (the blond one!). But as we know, that spark eventually does fade when your common sense kicks you in the pants. I thought, "Let's change this up and date someone with whom initially there is no spark, but hopefully after a few dates, there will be."

Maybe a lasting relationship happens for me when I gradually get to know the guy, and then eventually there will be fireworks. That's what happened with The Big One, and that worked for seven years. But there are not many environments I'm in where I can gradually get to know someone without dating him. Work, I guess, would be one place, but I prefer not dating someone in the workplace. That can end up as a recipe for disaster.

So, I met someone. He was not my type but passed all credentials one would look for in a suitor. He had a good job, a car and a condo; basically, he had his life together. I put on the ol' flirty charm, which resulted in him asking me out on a few dates. Mr. Safe Guy and I might actually have a shot. I thought I felt a spark. It wasn't a symphony of fireworks but it was better than nothing. I started wondering if this could lead to my first real boyfriend after The Big One. But then, the relationship got cut short because after a handful of dates, Mr. Safe Guy never called me again. What the @#!!**. I wanted to call him up and say, "Hey buddy, I didn't like you anyway. You were just an experiment and the experiment failed big-time! I don't even need to bake anything to get over you."

If you've ever been there, you sit down with your girlfriends and do what we do best: analyze the dilly out of the situation. Bewildered, you all come up with the only logical solution…someone has put a dating hex on you!!

MY FRIENDS THINK I'M CURSED,
WHITE CHOCOLATE BARK

anyone know any good witch doctors?

2½   **cups white chocolate chips**

1   **cup dried cranberries**

1   **cup of shelled pistachios (You can usually find these in the loose bulk section of your grocery store. Don't try to shell the salted ones; it's a lot of trouble and you usually eat most of them.)**

- ✪ Roast pistachios at 350°F (175°C) for 5–7 minutes.

- ✪ Melt chocolate over very low heat in a medium saucepan, stirring often. White chocolate is extremely sensitive. Take your time with it or it will turn into a big hard ball.

- ✪ Remove from heat; add cranberries and roasted pistachios.

- ✪ Spread mixture onto a lined cookie sheet. Let set then break into pieces.

CHAPTER 4
SINGLE & SASSY

NOW WHAT?!?!

I'M NOT BOY CRAZY, TOFFEE MAPLE SHORTBREAD

OKAY, SO MAYBE I AM A LITTLE. I'M ONLY HUMAN, YOU KNOW!!

¾	cup butter, softened
½	cup confectioners' sugar
1	tsp. maple extract
¼	tsp. salt
1¼	cups all-purpose flour
½	cup toffee baking bits

- ✪ Preheat oven to 300°F (150°C).

- ✪ Beat butter and confectioners' sugar together until light and fluffy.

- ✪ Add maple extract and salt; mix well.

- ✪ Stir in flour and toffee pieces; do not over mix.

- ✪ Put dough into an 8-inch square baking pan. Gently pat and even out dough.

- ✪ Bake for 35–40 minutes until top is golden brown, cool slightly, and then cut into squares.

BOY CRAZY?

My friends will tell you I'm boy crazy. Maybe I am a little.... I mean, I don't think about guys all the time.... Okay, so a couple of years ago I did check out the ambulance driver at a hospital. Since I had just broken my nose playing soccer, I probably did not look my best. My friend was laughing at me. Apparently, she felt holding a cold soda can on my swollen face with a bloody soccer jersey was not the best pick-up look. What is wrong with me? Could I really be that boy crazy? Maybe I do need to take a chill pill. Men are not everything, I keep reminding myself.

My happily single girlfriends tell me to relax and just enjoy being solo. Easy for them to say. They have pets, something to distract them from an empty apartment. Since I'm allergic to everything but fish, I don't have that option. I do have lots of plants (yes, I do talk to them), but they just don't give the same affection as a cute puppy...or a man...see, there I go again!

I get so confused. Lots of people have told me that love happens when you least expect it, so quit looking. Then, I read articles that say focus on what you want and it will happen. So, which is it? The universe is probably so confused that it doesn't know what to do with me. It's just keeping me on the back burner until I figure things out for myself, I guess.

Everyone says to spend more time with "me." So, I am. I'm taking belly-dancing classes. I'm learning to speak Spanish. I'm running 5k and 10k races. Although reconnecting with myself has enriched me in so many ways, it still hasn't made me think about men any less. Okay, maybe it has when I'm running a race and the only thing I'm focused on is reaching the finish line! It's funny. I catch myself trying not to check out guys as they walk by. "Just pretend like they are not there. Don't look at them." But what if the guy is really hot and checking me out? I can't let a single, handsome opportunity pass me by. SO, I check him out and realize quickly that he is so not cute. Arrgh! Maybe I need to wear blinders like the horses do. Apparently, DSquared designed some a couple of seasons back. If anyone has a pair, I may need to borrow them for the rest of my single life. Call me what you want: boy crazy, single and looking, cute and awesome—I can handle it.

WHERE HAVE ALL THE GOOD COWBOYS GONE COOKIE

seriously, i'm this close to moving to nashville!

¾ **cup sugar**
½ **cup brown sugar, packed**
½ **cup butter, softened**

1 **tsp. vanilla extract**
2 **eggs**

1¼ **cups all-purpose flour**
1 **cup quick-cooking oats**
1 **tsp. baking powder**
½ **tsp. baking soda**
½ **tsp. salt**

¾ **cup semisweet chocolate chips**
½ **cup peanuts**
15 **individual caramels,**
cut into small pieces

⚙ Preheat oven to 375°F (190°C).

⚙ In a large bowl, combine sugars with butter; beat until light and fluffy.

⚙ Add vanilla and eggs; blend well.

⚙ Add flour, oats, baking powder, baking soda and salt; mix well.

⚙ Stir in chocolate chips, peanuts and caramel pieces.

⚙ Roll into 1-inch balls. Place 2 inches apart on lined cookie sheet. Flatten with fingers. Bake for 10–12 minutes.

JUST ME, MYSELF AND PIE

SIMPLE AND AMAZING.

¼   **cup butter**
¼   **cup brown sugar**
1¼ **cups graham cracker crumbs (set aside 2 tbsps.)**

1   **package cooked chocolate pudding filling (not instant)**

◉ In a medium saucepan, melt together butter and brown sugar; mix well. Add graham cracker crumbs and press into a 9-inch pie plate.

◉ Prepare pie filling as directed on box. Pour on top of crust. Sprinkle with remaining graham cracker crumbs. Refrigerate until set (a few hours).

WHO NEEDS A MAN ON
VALENTINE'S DAY BISCOTTI

Perfect Replacement For a Date.

¾	cup butter, softened
1	cup sugar
2	eggs
1	tsp. vanilla extract
2½	cups all-purpose flour
1	tsp. cinnamon
1	tsp. baking powder
½	tsp. salt
1	cup flaked filberts (hazelnuts), roasted at 325°F (160°C) for 5–7 minutes.
¼	cup sugar
3	tsps. cinnamon; combine together for cinnamon sugar.

✪ Preheat oven to 350°F (175°C).

✪ In a medium bowl, mix together butter and sugar until light and fluffy. Beat in eggs and vanilla.

✪ In a separate bowl, sift the dry ingredients; mix into the wet mixture. Stir in the hazelnuts. (Dough will be thick.)

✪ Shape dough into 2 separate logs. Place logs on lined cookie sheet and flatten to ¾-inch thick logs. Sprinkle with cinnamon sugar.

✪ Bake for 30 minutes until set. Remove from oven and cool. When cool enough to touch, slice loaves into ½-inch slices. Place slices back on cookie sheet. Bake for an additional 5–7 minutes per side.

✪ Let cool and enjoy!

VALENTINE'S DAY/FELIZ DIA DE LOS ENAMORADOS

Another Valentine's Day, alone—no significant other! I don't care—I don't need some overpriced, overcrowded restaurant to feel loved. I'm more excited for it to be over so I can get some half-priced chocolate at Walmart.

Without fail, the one person who always sends me a Valentine's Day card is my mom with, of course, a lottery ticket inside. I'm not sure if it's a small-town thing, but we seem to give lottery tickets for every celebration.

I had just starting making biscotti. The hazelnuts were roasting in the oven. I sat down at my computer to check my lottery ticket. You need seven correct numbers to win the jackpot. I literally fell off my chair when I had matched six out of the seven numbers. I double- and triple-checked them. Holy moly, I had won something…how much? Not sure? All I knew was my hazelnuts were burning and the biscotti got put on hold.

Well, I won $1,400. I try to console myself at not having won much more by telling myself Yeah, that's $1,400 more than I had before, not OMG, I was just one digit away from being a millionaire. It was too little to save…maybe I should just be frivolous with it? Yep, that sounds about right. I had never been to a resort in a warm climate before. Most of my traveling had been with The Big One and since he didn't like resorts, we never went to one. We always had to go on "educational" vacations. I've been to art galleries in London, Spain, Germany, Italy and France, but I'm just not that into art. This time there would be no art galleries. All I wanted to learn was how long it would take me to swim up to the pool bar. I could definitely use some warm weather after a cold, snowy winter. Of course, I chose to take my mom, since she had bought me the ticket! So, we headed off to Cuba. Let the learning begin!

What happens in Cuba stays in Cuba. Well, except for this:

Since it was my first time at a resort, I didn't really know what to expect. I knew there would be gorgeous beaches for as long as the eye could see and unlimited mojitos and churros. What I didn't know was how much I would fall in love with the culture: the language, the music and especially the men. Everything felt so comfortable to me. Everyone really understood how to enjoy themselves and at a much slower pace than I was used to. It was also the first time I'd felt really confident with my figure. The men just love a woman with curves in all the right places. I felt as confident as Elle Macpherson, walking around in my tankini.

The first day of the trip, my curves and I strutted off to the hotel lobby for a group meeting on the different excursions the hotel offers. Well, there was one hot spot on my agenda that wasn't on their list…The Gardener. *Hola*, Orlando…Rolando, or something. It was like *Desperate Housewives* Cubano style. I took a short detour to check him out (late for the hotel meeting, of course). He had eyes as clear blue as the ocean and a killer bod (thanks to martial arts, I later learned). The dragon tattoo on his back drew even more attention to his smooth, tanned skin. We shared a glance and a greeting, and in that moment, I realized this would be a vacation that I would not soon forget.

After another day of shared glances and *holas*, he made his move. Since this was my first time at a resort, I didn't know the drill with the men there. First, he handed me a bouquet of flowers he'd put together himself, and I felt really special. Then, I noticed I wasn't so special because as I looked around, almost every woman of every shape, size and age had one—not necessarily made by my guy, but nonetheless I saw the pattern. Do the resorts have classes on bouquet making? Seriously, they're all really good at it.

I guess these guys have a system:

Step 1—Share flirty glances.

Step 2—The giving of the bouquet.

Step 3—They turn on the "make you feel special" charm; they have never met someone like you before or I think that's what he said in Spanish.

Step 4—You accidentally enter a dance competition in front of a couple hundred people because of too many mojitos (I came in second!).

Step 5—Secret midnight beach rendezvous. All done in one week, no strings attached. Okay, got it. I can handle this.

Can you blame him really? A week of fun in the sun with a cute foreigner you probably won't see again. I'm not gonna lie to you, I liked the attention. In my opinion, I got the cutest worker on the resort all to myself for one week. Then, I would pass my bouquet of flowers on to the next unsuspecting tourist who fancied my Cubano gardener.

Even though I knew my vacation love would be a short-term affair, I still could not stop from getting attached. My sun sign is Cancer, our nature is to love and be loved, and we can find reasons to get attached to the most unattainable men! We generally are very nurturing and affectionate. This is why I can never have a "friend with benefits." It just doesn't work.

I was thinking maybe I would come and visit him again. He was so good at making me feel special. I started to believe that I really am different. Or, maybe he'd had lots of practice at making people feel like one in a million. I was just his winning lottery ticket for the week. I wonder if they ever miss their vacation loves? Do they remember our names? Is there a special book of vacation love they enter our details in? Are we graded or just alphabetical? Ah, what the heck does it matter, when I kept calling my gardener the wrong name all week? But, then again, that didn't stop me from trying to figure out how I could fit him in my suitcase and take him home with me. By the end of the week I could tell that Orlando/Rolando had a wandering eye. Since I was leaving soon, he was already checking out his next possible chiquita. Wow, these guys are efficient. We exchanged addresses and phone numbers, but I knew we were just being polite.

After a long flight daydreaming about my love affair, I arrived back home to Toronto. Almost immediately, I picked up a how-to-speak-Spanish CD and dictionary. I learned to make mojitos and guacamole. Maybe I didn't come home with a husband, but it did open me up to a whole new culture. I've made a pact with myself to go away every winter. It's necessary. Not only does the warm weather do wonders for my mental stability during a long, cold season, but also the attention from the boys is great for my ego. I give that lesson an A+, not to mention an A+ to my Spanish teacher, the lovely and talented Rolando/Orlando! *Hasta luego!!*

WANTED

THE CHOCOLATE DESPERADOS

REWARD

SWEET TOOTH SATISFACTION

I WISH TIM McGRAW WA_ MY MAN,
DOUBLE CHOCOLATE BLONDIE

DON'T YOU THINK LIFE WOULD BE SWEETER IF HE WAS?

⅔ cup butter, softened

1½ cups brown sugar, packed

2 eggs

1½ tsps. vanilla extract

2 cups all-purpose flour

2 tsps. baking powder

½ tsp. salt

4 oz. milk chocolate, roughly chopped

4 oz. semisweet chocolate, roughly chopped

- Preheat oven to 350°F (175°C). Grease a 9 x 13-inch baking pan.

- Mix together butter and brown sugar until light and fluffy.

- Add eggs and vanilla; blend well.

- Stir in flour, baking powder and salt until just mixed.

- Stir in chocolate chunks and press into prepared pan.

- Bake for 20–25 minutes, until top is golden brown.

GETTING LUCKY AIN'T JUST FOR THE
IRISH CREAM CUPCAKES

I'M SINGLE NOT CELIBATE.

1½	cups all-purpose flour
1½	tsps. baking powder
¼	tsp. salt
½	cup butter, softened
1	cup sugar
2	large eggs, slightly beaten
1	tsp. vanilla extract
⅔	cup Irish cream liqueur

- Preheat oven to 350°F (175°C). Line cupcake tins. Makes 16–18.

- Stir together flour, baking powder and salt.

- In a separate bowl, cream together butter and sugar until light and fluffy.

- Add eggs and vanilla; mix well.

- Add a little flour mixture to butter mixture, alternating with Irish cream, mixing well after each addition. Beat until smooth.

- Fill muffin tins about ¾ full and bake for 18–20 minutes. Let cool before icing.

IRISH CREAM ICING

½	cup butter, softened
2	tbsps. Irish cream liqueur
2	cups confectioners' sugar

- Mix together butter and Irish cream; gradually add confectioners' sugar until you get a light and creamy texture.

TO DATE OR NOT TO DATE, BARK

MAYBE SINGLE AND SASSY IS THE NEW WAY TO GO?!?!

1   **10 oz. bar of 50% or 70% chocolate, cut into pieces**

1   **cup hazelnuts, roasted; crush into small and medium pieces**

²⁄₃   **cup dried blueberries**

✦ Melt chocolate in a medium saucepan over low heat. Remove from heat; stir in hazelnuts and blueberries. Spread onto a lined cookie sheet.

✦ Set in fridge; break into desired pieces.

SINGLE WOMEN
NEEDED FOR
taste test

1	**10 oz. bar of 50% or 70% chocolate, cut into pieces**
1	**tsp. peppermint extract**
12	**peppermint candy canes, crushed**
1/3	**cup white chocolate chips**
1	**tsp. vegetable oil**

☙ Melt chocolate in a medium saucepan over low heat. Remove from heat, add peppermint extract; stir well. Stir in half of the crushed candy canes. Spread onto a lined cookie sheet. Sprinkle with remaining candy canes.

☙ In a small saucepan over very low heat, melt white chocolate, add oil; stirring often. Drizzle over bark.

☙ Set in fridge; break into desired pieces.

133

TALL, DARK AND CARAMEL COOKIES

These cookies are a LOT LIKE THE PERFECT man:
rich and sweet…I'M KIDDING…well, sort of.

cup butter, softened
cup sugar
cup brown sugar, packed

egg
tsp. vanilla extract

cups all-purpose flour
tsp. baking soda
tsp. baking powder
tsp. salt

caramels, unwrapped
and cut into small pieces
(yes, you can eat one)

cup 50% dark
chocolate chips or 6 oz.
50% dark chocolate bar,
cut into small chunks

Preheat oven to 350°F (175°C).

In a large bowl, mix together
butter and sugars until light
and fluffy.

Add egg and vanilla; mix well.

In a medium bowl, sift together flour, baking
soda, baking powder,and salt. Blend flour
mixture into wet mixture until just blended.

Stir in caramels and chocolate chips.

Drop cookies by tablespoonfuls onto a lined
cookie sheet. Bake for 12–14 minutes.

MY LIFE CHART

This year, three of my closest friends got married, including my best friend and childhood confidante, Nikki Rae. When I say close friends, I mean that most of these people I have either known since I was three or since I moved to Toronto, in 1993. Four are pregnant—well, three. My former roommate just had her baby, the others are all due around the same time.

Wow, let's recap:	FRIENDS		ME
Marriages / Proposals	3		0…though, I did have 3 dates!
Pregnant		4	0…but practicing, safely!

In other words, I'm a little behind. It didn't really bother me, until Nikki Rae's wedding. My "Laverne" was moving on. Don't get me wrong, I was really happy for her; I strongly approved of her husband. But, I did feel a little lost. Before the wedding I'd been feeling so confident about being *single and sassy*. Then, I just started to feel alone like the single, lonesome black sheep. My "country" friends have been telling me they need to marry me off. What are they going to do, hold an auction? I remind them that I'm in a loving relationship with myself and that's all I need right now, which is mostly correct, minus the occasional lonely times. I'm not sure if they buy it but I really don't expect just any man to fill that empty feeling I have. I need to fill it. And not always with cupcakes and cookies, though they seem to do the trick temporarily. At least my family doesn't mingle in my personal life. My mom still dislikes all men and has a hate-on for marriage. I think she likes being my date for functions, so at least someone's okay with my singledom.

I try to remind myself that all the great things in my life are like a fruit basket—my family, my friends, my career, my condo. I'd hate to seem desperate like some guys I've met online who say, "Lonely guy looking for a great gal to make his life better," or something sad like that. I think I have my own issues, so why the heck do I want to take on someone else's? I certainly wouldn't want to put that pressure on someone I was dating. My future man should add to my fruit-filled life. Yes, my "life" fruit basket—it's full of some staples and more exotic fruits. I would like to add a mango or a good old staple fruit like an apple. But in no way should any man take from my basket.

After having time off during the spring, I've become a lot more comfortable with myself. I fill my social calendar with things I want to do, not just activities to distract me from the fact I'm single. I no longer feel bitter toward any of my friends who were becoming pregnant and getting married. I am truly happy for them. The area of emptiness inside me is feeling smaller and smaller. My "life" fruit basket has become pretty full and I've done it all on my own.

Little did I know I'd fall out of the basket with a relapse at Nikki Rae's wedding. Maybe it was because I'd had too much champagne, but as I watched my "Laverne" walk down that aisle I started wondering, when is it my turn to feel uncomfortable at wedding/ baby showers? I want everyone staring at me as I open presents. When do I get to have my Bridezilla moments (I think I would be good at it)? When do I get to wear maternity pants? They seem highly functional, especially for buffets.

So, whenever I feel a moment of doubt, I remind myself that I am special—one of a kind. This feeling will pass. I tell myself tomorrow is a new day and everything is going to be okay. Just because I'm on my own doesn't make me defective goods. One day I will meet someone to join me in my fruit-filled life. One day, I might be the best Bridezilla ever (kidding, I'm not that bitchy). Some people might call me picky. I don't think I'm picky. I just know what I want. I've always been that way, right from my first pair of pleather pants. It might be hard to find a matching pair of pleather pants, but I know it will happen. Until that day comes, I'll just keep filling up on fruit. And whenever I put too much pressure on myself, I remember the words my dear Gramps would say that helped me through many experiences, "Don't take life too seriously, you will never get out of it alive."

ME AND MY RICE PUDDING ARE JUST FINE ON OUR OWN, THANK YOU

THIS RECIPE IS JUST AS POPULAR IN THE COUNTRY AS IT IS IN THE CITY. IT'S NOT SHORT ON COMFORTING, EITHER.

½ **cup uncooked long-grain rice, prepare as directed.**

3 **cups milk, 1% or 2%**
⅓ **cup sugar**
2 **eggs, beaten**
1 **tsp. vanilla extract**
½ **tsp. cinnamon**

- ✪ In a heavy-bottom saucepan, cook the rice as directed.

- ✪ Preheat oven to 350°F (175°C).

- ✪ Whisk together milk, sugar, beaten eggs, vanilla and cinnamon. Stir in cooked rice.

- ✪ Pour into a 2-quart baking dish.

- ✪ Bake for 30 minutes; stir. Cook, for another 20–30 minutes or until pudding is set but a little jiggly.

- ✪ Let cool and refrigerate.

Singles ✦
seal of approval

ALWAYS A BRIDESMAID, NANAIMO BARS

IT'S GIVEN ME GOOD PRACTICE. I'VE GOT THIS WEDDING THING
DOWN PAT...EXCEPT FOR THE MARRIAGE PART.

BASE:

½	cup butter
¼	cup sugar
⅓	cup cocoa
1	egg
1¾	cups graham cracker crumbs
¾	cup coconut

FILLING:

½	cup butter, softened
3	tbsps. milk
1	tsp. vanilla
2	tbsps. custard powder or instant vanilla pudding mix
2	cups confectioners' sugar

GLAZE:

3	tbsps. butter
¾	cup semisweet chocolate chips

These are no-bake squares.

BASE:
In a medium saucepan, combine butter, sugar and cocoa; stir well. Add egg; cook and stir constantly over medium-low heat until mixture thickens. Remove from heat. Mix in graham cracker crumbs and coconut. Press into a greased 8- or 9-inch-square pan. Chill.

FILLING:
In a mixing bowl, beat together butter, milk, vanilla, custard powder and confectioners' sugar; until light and fluffy. Spread evenly over base. Chill.

GLAZE:
In a small saucepan over low heat, melt butter and chocolate chips. Let cool slightly. Pour evenly over filling. Refrigerate.

MY EGGS ARE NOT GETTING ANY YOUNGER CRÈME BRÛLÉE

I STILL HAVE A FEW YEARS BEFORE I SHOULD PROBABLY FREEZE MY EGGS. UNTIL THEN, I WILL MAKE THIS WHENEVER I FEEL MY CLOCK TICKING.

3	cups 35% whipping cream
8	egg yolks
½	cup sugar
1	pinch salt
2	tsps. vanilla extract
6	tbsps. sugar

- ✪ Preheat oven to 300°F (150°C). Makes 6 servings.

- ✪ In heavy-bottom saucepan, over medium-low heat, heat the cream until bubbles just start to form around the edges of the pot.

- ✪ Meanwhile, in a bowl, whisk together the egg yolks, ½ cup sugar, salt and vanilla until the mixture is pale yellow.

- ✪ When the cream is ready, pour it very slowly into the egg mixture as you whisk briskly. Make sure that you are constantly whisking as you add the cream; otherwise the egg will cook and the mixture will separate.

- ✪ When the mixture is thoroughly combined, pour it through a fine strainer to remove any small lumps.

- ✪ Pour the brûlée mixture evenly into ramekins and place in a water bath (a large baking pan with hot water). Fill hot water halfway up around the ramekins. Bake for approximately 1 hour, or until the brûlée is just set when jiggled.

- ✪ Let brûlée sit at room temperature for about 15 minutes, then chill in refrigerator for at least a couple of hours before serving.

- ✪ To serve, sprinkle each with 1 tbsp. sugar and caramelize using a crème brûlée torch, or under a hot broiler (for 2–3 minutes).

SO YOU ARE THE LAST ONE LEFT TO GET MARRIED AND HAVE A BABY S'MORE

when you know you want some more out of life.

⅔	cup sugar
½	cup butter, softened
½	tsp. vanilla extract
1	egg
2⅓	cups graham cracker crumbs
⅓	cup flour
½	tsp. salt
3	cups mini marshmallows
1½	tbsps. butter
2	cups semisweet chocolate chips
1½	cups mini marshmallows

✪ Preheat oven to 350°F (175°C).

✪ In a mixing bowl, beat sugar and butter until light and fluffy. Add vanilla and egg; mix well. Stir in graham cracker crumbs, flour and salt.

✪ Set aside 1½ cups of this mixture. Put the remaining crumb mixture in a greased 9 x 13-inch pan.

✪ Melt 3 cups of mini marshmallows with 1½ tbsps. of butter in a small saucepan. Spread evenly over base. Sprinkle chocolate chips, 1½ cups marshmallows and remaining graham cracker crumb mixture on top; press lightly.

✪ Bake for 17–22 minutes or until marshmallows puff up slightly and are golden brown. Let cool.

WOW, I'M STILL SINGLE IN THE CITY, MUNCHIES

THIS RECIPE IS PERFECT WHEN YOU WANT SOMETHING a LITTLE SWEET AND SALTY.

2	12 oz. bags of milk chocolate chips
1	9.5 oz. bag of corn chips (like Fritos), crushed

- In a large saucepan over low heat, melt chocolate chips.

- Remove from heat; stir in crushed corn chips.

- Drop by teaspoonful or melon baller onto alined cookie sheet. Let cool in the fridge. I store the cookies in a freezer bag in my fridge.

I JUST BOUGHT MY FIRST CONDO BECAUSE I'M STILL SINGLE
CARAMEL SHORTBREAD

sharing a mortgage is overrated. I play my country music as loud as I want now. yee haw!!

BASE:
⅔	cup butter, softened
¼	cup sugar
1¼	cups all-purpose flour

FILLING:
½	cup butter
½	cup packed light brown sugar
2	tbsps. light corn syrup
½	cup sweetened condensed milk

TOPPING:
1¼	cups semisweet chocolate chips

✪ Preheat oven to 350°F (175°C).

✪ In a medium bowl, mix together butter, sugar and flour until crumbly. Press into an 8-inch-square pan. Bake for 20 minutes.

✪ In a medium heavy-bottom saucepan, combine butter, brown sugar, corn syrup and sweetened condensed milk. Bring to a boil. Boil for 5 minutes. Remove from heat and beat by hand for a couple of minutes. Pour evenly over baked crust. Let the caramel firm.

✪ Melt chocolate over low heat in a small saucepan. Pour evenly over caramel layer. Chill, then cut into squares. This recipe is very rich, so I cut it into small squares.

NO MONEY NO HONEY, BUTTER TARTS

REALLY I'M NOT ASKING FOR MUCH: JUST A MAN WITH A JOB, A CAR, <u>SINGLE</u>, CUTE—OH—AND ANATOMICALLY CORRECT. APPARENTLY, IT'S A TALLER ORDER THAN I THINK!

1	package of flaky pie crust mix, (prepare as directed)
1	cup packed brown sugar
1/3	cup butter, melted
2	tbsps. milk
1	egg, beaten
1	tbsp. pure maple syrup
½	tsp. vanilla extract
3	tbsps. coconut

- Preheat oven to 375°F (190°C).

- Separate dough into 12 firm balls. Flatten each ball and roll out to fit in muffin tins.

- In a small bowl, combine brown sugar and butter; mix well. Add milk, beaten egg, maple syrup and vanilla; stir well.

- Place 1 tsp. of coconut in the bottom of each tart shell. Pour mixture on top of coconut to fill muffin tins about 2/3 full. Bake for 18–20 minutes. Let cool.

VACATION BOYFRIEND #2

My dating tales wouldn't be complete without my latest escapade. With some time on my hands this winter, I decided I was due for another warm getaway, since the last one had gone so well! As a single gal, with every close friend either engaged or pregnant, I thought of actually going alone. But, even though I'm quite independent, I still find that idea a little scary. What if I were to have too many mojitos and run into some hooligans? I am a lot of fun on my own, but without some liquid courage, I can be quite shy. I decided that vacationing solo just wouldn't work. So, I phoned up my cousin TJ in England and said, "Can you book us a trip somewhere warm in Europe?" Sick of the endless English rain, she was all over it. She needed some Vitamin D pronto. So, off I was to England, then to the Canary Islands. *HOLA!!* Sangria and paella, here I come.

At least this time if I were to meet someone I'd know the drill: The meet-and-greet… check. The bouquet of flowers…check. The midnight beach rendezvous…check. I did think I'd leave out the dance competition this time. All done in one week, no strings attached.

From rain and snow to sun and sand, there we were on a beautiful Spanish island. TJ and I loved that we were the only two Canadians there. Talk about getting attention! Free champagne, food, gifts. Wow, celebrity treatment! I think we caused a few cases of whiplash.

Our first night on the Island, TJ and I decided to hit the village. I think I had been unwillingly groped by a European from every country. I was losing my faith in men altogether. I'd thought to myself, was this it? I was thirtysomething while everyone else was twentysomething and with busy, unruly hands. I mean, I don't mind busy hands but not when they don't know what they are doing and have no class. I was honestly upset and thought am I ever going to find someone to have a real relationship with? Or am I just stuck with Hans Busy Hands? I know the bar may not be the likeliest place to meet one's potential future husband, but in my opinion it's just as good a place as anywhere. I've always figured if I'm at the bar and I'm not a player, then there has to be a male counterpart like me.

The next morning, tired and hung over, TJ and I decided to recuperate on the beach in the glorious sunshine. Nothing cures a hangover like the sound of the ocean and the warm sun on your back. We were reminiscing about the last night's events with laughter and a bit of horror. Then we decided it was time for a much needed greasy lunch and a little hair of the dog. As we ventured out on our quest for burgers and fries I saw him, my vacation boyfriend, "Mr. I Think I Could Get Used to You!" He had the most gorgeous tanned skin, short brown hair and a very kind face with dimples. His smile could light up the whole island. I saw him first from the *playa* (beach), as I did my infamous Elle Macpherson strut (yes, I can still do it hungover) right up to the entry of his family's beachside restaurant, where he was working. Of course it happened again. My weakness for hot Spanish men, that is. I began to visualize our children, already redecorating his place in my head. Even before we had muttered a sentence to each other, I could feel the attraction was instant and mutual. Could someone actually be that perfect? TJ and I sat down at his restaurant. He took our orders. I asked (in my head) if he was on the menu. That damn romance language gets me every time; it just sounds so alluring. He could have been telling me off and I'd think he was professing his love for me.

Although our beer, sangria and greasy food hit the spot, he was definitely the most memorable part of my meal. His English was pretty good and we chatted as best we could, but mostly we let our eyes do the talking. TJ and I asked him where the hottest nightspots were. He wrote down a few and asked us when we were going out. We said the next day. Well, it just happened to be his thirtieth birthday, and he asked if he and his friends could tag along with us. "Hell, yeah!"

Well, Hans would have to grope someone else. Because that day I had met a man who made me believe that decent men do exist. I could tell he had class and respect for women. It was in the way people treated him. They liked him. His momma had raised him right. He said it was destiny that we'd met for his birthday. Who doesn't want to hear that? I told him that my psychic had told me all about him (kidding). Anyway, though I may not have been sure about the destiny thing, I knew we were destined to have an amazing time celebrating his thirtieth.

The next day he arrived at our bungalow in the evening with gifts: chocolate, wine and rum…the man actually brought us gifts on his birthday. I thought maybe they do things backward here in Spain but then realized, nope, he is just as sweet as pie (mmm, pie!). After a few hours of charades trying to understand each other, we were off to the local bar area. I hadn't heard this much eighties music since, well…the eighties. TJ and I actually swayed to "We Are the World." Nothing says Kasbah like "Summer of '69." Bryan Adams is like a God in this place. We partied until 5:00 a.m. Not the best thing to do when the next morning you are booked on a winding bus tour around a volcano to visit a rum factory.

For the rest of the week, my vacation boyfriend made our trip something I will not soon forget. I felt instantly comfortable with him, as though we'd met before in a past life. We were always welcome at his restaurant. He gave us unlimited food and drink and we didn't have to pay a dime. I didn't think gentlemen like that still existed. Ladies, I know when you go away there can be a lot of players but I know he wasn't like that. He didn't even seem to know the checklist. I could tell he didn't do this often. Actions speak louder than words, and his actions were nothing short of great. He was always lending a helping hand, giving lollipops to screaming toddlers, assisting elderly people up a ramp on the beach walkway, taking coffee to the people working in the nearby pharmacy, all done with a smile on his face.

Ah, my Knight in Shining Armor, he even owned an Arabian horse. He didn't accidentally throw his mocha latte all over me, but I still wanted to ride off into the sunset with him, romantically speaking broken languages to each other. Sure, the language barrier can be difficult. But if you are like me, sometimes you wish you couldn't understand all the "BS" your guy was telling you and would rather he show you how much he really means what he is saying. Every day he would tell me he would come to visit me in the summer, "Sure, sure," I'd say. He could tell that I didn't believe him. Come on, a relationship with a guy that is a ten-hour flight away? Do long distance relationships actually work? Really, I need some space but maybe not that much. I've had relationships with guys, but because our work schedules were completely different, I wouldn't even see them for weeks, even if we lived only a ten-minute drive apart. Who knew, maybe it could actually work. His father would say to him, "Canada, oh too many kilometers." But it didn't seem to faze my Vacation Boyfriend. The last day of my trip was as good as the first. His eyes did not wander; he gave me his undivided attention. Because he was working and couldn't drive us to the airport, he insisted on giving us cab fare. Sweet, right up to the end. We said our *Hasta luegos* and off I went home.

So, he is supposed to come and visit in a couple of months. Yes, I will be disappointed if he doesn't. That doesn't change the fact that I had an amazing vacation. I haven't smiled at a man's picture this much since my Joey McIntyre poster. I'm trying not to look at the negative side of my dating escapades anymore. He might be Mr. Perfect For Me, or he might have been Mr. Perfect For My Vacation. Either way, I wouldn't have changed a single thing, except for the ten pounds I'm trying to shed. I'm going to look so hot, he won't know what hit him. IF he comes to visit. In the meantime, I'll daydream about spending the rest of my life with my hot Spanish man on a beautiful island...yeah, I could get used to that.

SPICY DARK CHOCOLATE ISLAND BARK

Because my vacation boyfriend is coming in two months.

1   cup whole almonds (skin on)

1   10 oz. bar of 70% dark chocolate
2   8 oz. bars of 99.9% dark chocolate
       (Dark chocolate has less sugar.)

1½   tsps. cinnamon

½   tsp. cayenne pepper

- Preheat oven to 350°F (175°C).

- Place nuts on a cookie sheet and roast in oven for 5–7 minutes.

- Cut the large bar of chocolate into medium-sized pieces. Break the two 99.9% bars into pieces. Melt chocolate over low heat in a medium saucepan.

- Add spices to chocolate when melted. Stir in nuts. Spread mixture onto a cookie sheet and place in freezer to set.

- When set, break in pieces and store in a freezer bag. I love to keep bark in the freezer; it tastes amazing when it's cold.

- I eat chocolate every day when I am trying to shed a couple of pounds. I eat small amounts of this. It has less sugar because of the dark chocolate. Cinnamon and cayenne pepper have amazing health benefits and nuts add protein.

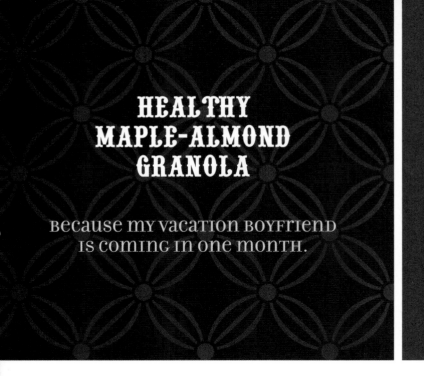

HEALTHY MAPLE-ALMOND GRANOLA

Because my vacation boyfriend is coming in one month.

½	cup Grade B pure maple syrup
2	tbsps. unpasturized honey
1	tbsp. vegetable oil
2	tsps. cinnamon
¼	tsp. nutmeg
1	tsp. vanilla extract
½	cup flaxseed meal
2	cups quick cooking oats
1	cup slivered or whole almonds
½	cup unsweetened coconut
1	cup dark 50% chocolate chips

- Preheat oven to 300°F (150°C). Grease a 13 x 9-inch baking pan.

- In a medium saucepan over medium-low heat, combine maple syrup, honey, oil, cinnamon and nutmeg. Bring to a boil. Remove from heat; stir in vanilla. Stir in flaxseed meal, oats, almonds and coconut. Pour into prepared pan.

- Bake for 35–45 minutes or until golden brown, stirring every 15–20 minutes. Granola will crisp up when cooled. Add dark chocolate chips when granola is thoroughly cooled.

- This is great as a snack, or added to plain yogurt topped with fresh fruit and honey. I never seem to get sick of it, and it's pretty good for you, too.

- Cool; store in an airtight container.

After all the Internet dating, speed dating, dating events, vacations, blind dates, etc., I'm wondering what's next for this single, pretty cute, independent woman living in the city?

I get more and more confident and happy with the person I am each day. Sure, I have my moments of anxiety where I think I will be single forever and have actually looked into freezing my eggs. What if I don't find Mr. Right for Me? There are times when I miss cuddling with someone on the couch, having a date for weddings, etc. It's taken me a long time and a baker's dozen worth of experiences to know one thing for sure: I would rather be alone and happy than with someone just for the sake of not being alone.

I might be a bit guarded now when it comes to dealings with the heart, but I am still willing to give it a shot. I would hope my future Mr. Right for Me would do the same. Maybe I've already met him. Maybe we've passed each other on the street. Maybe I won't meet him for ten years because he's on a secret mission for the government.

Whatever the case, I can rest assured there will be a lot of dating and happy baking for this single and sassy woman.

RECIPE INDEX